RAKE & ROMANCE

THE BEAUCROFT GIRLS
BOOK TWO

SUZANNE G. ROGERS

IDUNN COURT PUBLISHING

Idunn Court Publishing
7 Ramshorn Court
Savannah, GA 31411

Published by Idunn Court Publishing, January 2016

Editor: Kathryn Riley Miller
Cover Design: Suzanne G. Rogers

❋ Created with Vellum

CONTENTS

STRANGE REQUEST

Late July, 1845, London, England

As the carriage rolled through the streets of London at a brisk clip, Juliet and her mother were obliged to hang on to the straps overhead to avoid sliding to the floor. When one of the wheels hit a particularly large bump, Mrs. Beaucroft made a sound of disgust.

"This is your father's fault, you know. I can't believe he kept the carriage out so late this afternoon, especially when he knew you and I had been invited to a soirée."

"We're only a little late for the party, Mama. If it was that important to you to arrive on time, we could have hired a carriage."

"Nobody who's anybody arrives to a party in a hired carriage, dear." A smile replaced the frown. "When you're Lady Elbourne, I daresay you'll have your pick of carriages."

"Mama, I beg you not to go on about that. Augustus and I get on together swimmingly, but he's given me no indication he's about to propose."

Mrs. Beaucroft seemed to pay her no heed. "I'm rather vexed

at him, I must say. We've very few social events left in the Season, and he's not even going to be at the soirée tonight."

"Since his papa summoned him home, it's hardly his fault. I do hope nothing's wrong."

"Lord Moregate would have said something in his message if anything had been terribly wrong."

"I suppose so."

"At any rate, if Augustus doesn't propose soon, we'll have very little time to revel in your triumph before the Season ends."

Juliet made no response other than to stare out the window. If truth be told, she partly agreed with her mother. Although she wasn't at all annoyed with Augustus, she *was* looking forward to becoming engaged to the most eligible bachelor of the Season. Wouldn't all the naysayers who said she couldn't hold a candle to her sister get their comeuppance! In addition, the gown she was wearing that evening was a particular favorite of hers, and she was disappointed the earl wouldn't have the chance to see it. The darts in the white silk bodice made her waist look exceptionally small, and the cornflower blue embroidery on the full overskirt went well with her porcelain complexion and toffee-colored hair. Oh, well, perhaps she could wear it for him another time.

At Lord and Lady Ayscoghe's soirée, Juliet left Mrs. Beaucroft chatting with a gaggle of matrons and went in search of someone her own age. The gathering was filled with all manner of pleasant and well-heeled company, but she suddenly felt the absence of her sister more keenly than ever before. Kitty had been her near constant companion all her life, so Juliet had almost never been alone. Her sister had married recently, however, and was living with her new husband, Lord Philip, in the country. Philip's elder brother, Augustus, could usually be relied upon for amiable conversation, but he was absent tonight. Perhaps it was *his* comforting presence she missed most of all.

Before Juliet had gone more than a few steps, Lady Lovejoy

descended. As usual, the widowed countess was clad in an exquisite couture gown of the finest materials, undoubtedly acquired during one of her frequent jaunts to Paris.

"Come with me, my dear. I've something I must speak with you about."

The countess maneuvered her into an alcove, where they had a modicum of privacy.

"First of all, I've have had it from very good sources that your former friend, Miss Haver, is completely ruined to all good society."

The way the woman said the word *ruined* left absolutely nothing to the imagination, and Juliet was dismayed. "Are you quite sure?"

"Her parents have disowned her, and there can be no more reliable confirmation than that."

Since Violet Haver had tried to interfere with Kitty's courtship, Juliet had several excellent reasons for holding a grudge. Nevertheless, she wasn't so hard-hearted as to rejoice in her misery.

"I'm dreadfully sorry to hear it. Despite Violet's missteps, I don't wish her ill. I suppose her ruination is Lord Gryphon's doing?"

"You've supposed correctly. That knave has been responsible for the downfall of more than one foolish girl, although usually not a girl as highly placed as Miss Haver. He's such a reprobate, nobody will receive him any longer. In fact, his grandfather, Lord Harkencester, is so disgusted with that entire branch of the family, he's decided to settle the estate on his younger son, Lord Horatio."

On that score, Juliet had little trouble believing the countess. Indeed, she held a far less charitable view of Lord Gryphon than she held of Violet, and possessed an even larger grudge. The viscount had tried to take liberties with Kitty, and only the timely intervention of Lord Philip had salvaged her reputation.

If Lord Gryphon had been financially and socially disadvantaged, it was because he deserved it.

"Lord Gryphon will still inherit the title of marquess someday, won't he?"

"Yes, but otherwise he's been cut off without a penny. His parents, Lord and Lady Kesselbury, are still received, but Lord Gryphon can find no ready welcome anywhere. It's a sad situation, really."

"And to think, Lord Gryphon once sought Kitty's hand in marriage!"

"Your sister is much better off where she is, despite her rather unconventional courtship with Lord Philip. At any rate, this brings me to my request. Lord Horatio has just returned to England with the goal of getting his daughter married off. He's been living in Texas these past seventeen years, and made a vast fortune of his own in cattle."

Juliet was impressed. "How very clever of him."

"Yes, it's never easy for a second son to make his way in the world. Lord Horatio is looking for a London home, but in the meantime, he and his family are staying with me. Will you take his daughter under your wing so she has at least one friend in town? I'd consider it a personal favor."

Although she managed to keep her countenance, Juliet's heart sank. She'd rather throw herself into a thorny rose bush than have anything to do with Lord Gryphon's relatives, but she wouldn't dream of saying so. "Why, I'd be glad to befriend Miss Gryphon. I was just thinking how lonely it is for me without Kitty around."

"I knew you'd be willing to help. Miss Gryphon is an attractive girl, apart from her dreadful foreign accent and manners. Unfortunately, she's been unfairly tainted by association with her notorious cousin. If you and I befriend her, however, the stain may be somewhat ameliorated."

Although Juliet smiled, she wasn't so sure she agreed. Her

own family would most certainly be appalled by anyone bearing the name of Gryphon. Nevertheless, Lady Lovejoy was an influential member of society, and her requests were rarely refused.

"I'll do what I can, naturally."

"Lord Horatio expects his daughter to make an excellent match, so your alliance with Miss Gryphon will stand you in good stead going forward." The countess giggled. "What am I saying? Considering your close relationship with Lord Elbourne, you're hardly in need of any assistance in society."

Although the implication brought color to Juliet's cheeks, she pretended not to understand. "Indeed, Augustus has been a splendid friend."

"Don't be so modest! All society is awaiting the announcement of your engagement to the earl."

"I hate to disappoint anyone, but no such announcement is forthcoming." Augustus hadn't yet proposed, so Juliet could hardly give any other response. Furthermore, it was better to heighten the suspense by denying the truth of the matter. When she was ready to make the announcement, her triumph would be that much greater. "Is Miss Gryphon here this evening?"

"Yes, but she's playing billiards with the gentlemen."

"No!" Juliet's hands flew to her mouth and her eyes widened in horror.

"I'm afraid so. I suggested she circulate, but she seemed intent on her game."

"Doesn't Miss Gryphon understand the proper way to behave in London society?"

"Alas, her mother perished when the child was only twelve. Lord Horatio assures me his daughter learned all the proper graces at a girls' boarding school in America." She wrinkled her nose. "Only heaven knows what she'll have to unlearn, but I'm sure you'll be an excellent influence."

"I'll do my best."

Despite her assertion, Juliet wasn't entirely sure if her best would be good enough. After all, she'd failed to save poor Violet from disaster. To be fair, however, her former friend had never sought her help.

Lady Lovejoy beckoned. "Come with me and I'll introduce you."

~

Meadow's End, Derbyshire England

As soon as the dapper Earl of Elbourne entered his father's study, the distinct odor of brandy assailed his nostrils. Since the Marquess of Moregate wasn't ordinarily a heavy drinker, Augustus suspected something dreadful had occurred. One glance at his father's countenance confirmed it.

"What's happened, Father? Why did you call me back from London?"

"I've bad news, I'm afraid." The older man seemed to be enveloped in a cloud of despair.

"You'd best tell me. Perhaps I can help."

"That's why I summoned you." Moregate swallowed a quantity of amber liquid, but it didn't seem to lift his mood. "You mentioned Miss Beaucroft a great deal in your letters."

"Y-Yes." Augustus was bewildered. How could sweet Juliet possibly have anything to do with his father's problems? "My regard for her grows daily."

"Have you made her an offer of marriage?"

"Not yet."

"Thank heavens." His father drew in a deep breath and let it out. "I'm not too late."

"I'm not sure what you mean. I'm planning to speak with her father just before the Season ends."

"I'm sorry, but it's out of the question. You and Miss Beaucroft can never marry."

His father's pronouncement hung in the air like a cloud of cigar smoke. When Augustus first received his father's vague summons, he left London without delay, expecting to discover his signature was required on a document or some other bit of urgent business had arisen which could be dealt with swiftly. He meant to deal with the problem and return to Juliet's side to finish the last few weeks of the Season, but it appeared as if his father had lost his mind instead.

Augustus peered at him. "You look rather ill. Perhaps one of the servants should fetch a physician."

"It would be more useful to call a banker, I'm afraid." The marquess rubbed his bleary, bloodshot eyes. "Let me speak plainly, so we have no misunderstanding. Our family is in the midst of an economic calamity and we're very close to becoming insolvent."

Augustus's knees buckled and he sank into a chair. "How can this have happened so suddenly? I understand Grovebrook was distressed when you sold it to Philip, but I thought most of our other properties were in the black!"

His father sighed. "The truth of the matter is that I'm abominably bad at managing my assets, and I've placed my faith in the most undeserving and dishonest people. After Philip disclosed how badly Mr. Pratt had cheated me out of any profits from Grovebrook, I took a closer look at my financial affairs. What I discovered mortified and humbled me."

Augustus's eyes widened. "How bad is it?"

"Even if we sell every underperforming asset, the estate will still be losing money. I've hired a new man of business—Mr. Burton Kelly—who'll be implementing several positive improvements. If we're very fortunate, we may turn things around...but not without a huge infusion of cash."

"I can scarcely believe it."

His father gestured toward the array of papers and books spread out on his desk. "I encourage you to review the economic mess I've made. Perhaps there's some aspect I've overlooked."

"Yes, I'll begin right away. Also, I'll speak with Mr. Kelly about his plans for improvements as soon as possible. We must err on the side of caution, I think."

"Be that as it may, Augustus, let me be blunt; if you don't marry a very wealthy heiress in the next few months, our finances will collapse and your inheritance will be worth only a small fraction of what it's worth today. We'll most certainly be forced to sell Meadow's End."

Augustus gaped. "Mother couldn't withstand the strain of leaving this house!"

"We'll do everything in our power to avoid losing our home. In the meantime, she has no idea about this financial catastrophe, and I'd like it to remain that way."

"Of course."

Although it was only midafternoon, Augustus poured himself a glass of whiskey from the sideboard and drained it. "I confess, this news has come as a shock. Ours wouldn't be the only wealthy family ever forced to acknowledge economic reality, I suppose, but I'd had no idea we were foundering this badly."

The marquess stared into his brandy, looking older than his years. "Forgive me, lad. I should have been a better steward of our estate, and I'm deeply sorry."

"We'll straighten it all out, Father."

Despite his optimistic words, Augustus was deeply worried. Furthermore, he was distraught about Juliet Beaucroft. As the future Marquess of Moregate, he'd been expected to make a good match. Up until now, he'd assumed he had enough financial leeway to choose a bride of modest means and background. He and Juliet were so congenial together, and so well-suited, he'd easily envisioned a life of marital harmony with her by his side. Unless he wished to completely turn his back on family obligation, however the choice was out of his hands.

He swallowed a lump of disappointment. "Have you written to Philip?"

"Not yet. Newly married, with Grovebrook to manage, I didn't feel it was fair to burden him right now. Nevertheless, he should be informed before too long."

"I don't know how I'm going to break this news to Juliet."

"I thought you hadn't yet proposed?"

"I haven't, but I've given her every reason to assume I will. Since Philip's marriage to her sister, I've come to view Juliet as my closest confidant."

"Miss Beaucroft will always be your friend and confidant, but she can't be your wife. For what it's worth, she's a dear girl and your mother and I are fond of her." Moregate cleared his throat. "Now, we must discuss your marital prospects."

"What if I can't find a wealthy woman to wed in time to save our finances?"

"As it so happens, a childhood acquaintance of mine has a daughter of marriageable age. Lord Horatio suggested the match a year ago, but I'd dismissed the notion out of hand until now. You see, although the girl was born in England, she's resided in North America for most of her life."

"You've always had contempt for Americans!" Augustus stared at the marquess, aghast.

"It's a fine distinction, I grant you, but she's been residing in the Republic of Texas." His father slid him an apologetic glance. "There's something else you should know; Lord Horatio is Lord Gryphon's uncle."

"You *must* be joking!"

"Desperate times call for desperate measures, lad."

"To be related to Zachary Gryphon, even by marriage, is insupportable." Augustus shook his head. "There must be some other lady to consider."

"None who come to mind."

"No, this is absolutely absurd. I refuse."

"Why don't you meet Miss Gryphon before you reject her? I was at Horatio's wedding, and I can attest to the fact her mother, Rebecca, was an extraordinary beauty. No doubt the girl is equally lovely."

"No one could ever hold a candle to Juliet Beaucroft. That's my final word."

THE COUNTESS LED Juliet into a game room filled with masculinity and cigar smoke. Several gentlemen were occupied with cards at corner tables, but others were more actively employed in a game of billiards. As Juliet watched, a beautiful brunette leaned over the green felt-covered table and tapped in a bank shot requiring obvious skill. The surrounding players erupted into admiring applause.

Lady Lovejoy bent her head closer to Juliet's ear. "That's Miss Stephanie Gryphon."

"She's very pretty."

"I quite agree. Few young ladies could rival your sister in looks, but Miss Gryphon might come close."

A particular young gentleman seated at one of the card tables drew Juliet's notice. He resembled Lord Gryphon so completely, she believed it to be the viscount at first. But after she'd studied the man a few moments, his demeanor and facial expressions revealed him to be another person entirely.

"Lady Lovejoy, is that gentleman sitting over there Mr. Gryphon?"

The countess followed her glance. "Indeed, it is. The family resemblance between Mr. Cody Gryphon and Lord Gryphon is remarkable."

Juliet nodded. "I could almost mistake one for the other."

"The older gentleman seated directly across from young Mr. Gryphon is his father, Lord Horatio." The countess patted her coiffure "He's a handsome devil as well."

"Yes, he is."

"Just between us, he was my beau many years ago. Truth be told, I still have a soft spot for the man."

Juliet's gaze was drawn once more to Cody. Her appreciation for his brooding good looks was immediately followed by a pang of guilt. Augustus was quite handsome, inside and out, and she hoped to make the earl her husband. Therefore, she had no business admiring another man—even from afar. She averted her eyes before anyone noticed her staring. It wouldn't do for her to appear interested.

Since the billiards game had concluded, Lady Lovejoy seized her chance. "Excuse me, Miss Gryphon? I'd like to introduce you to a friend of mine."

"Why certainly!" Stephanie set her cue down and glided over.

The countess immediately ushered both girls from the room. "Miss Stephanie Gryphon, this is Miss Juliet Beaucroft."

Juliet curtsied. "It's a pleasure to meet you."

Stephanie dipped into a curtsy of her own. "Likewise."

"I'll leave you two young people to get better acquainted. I'm sure you have a great deal in common." Lady Lovejoy hastened off.

Juliet inhaled fresh air to clear her lungs of smoke. "I'll never understand how men stand the stench of cigars."

"I enjoy it, actually." Stephanie's strange accent was somewhat jarring. "But then I'm more accustomed to the company of men than women. Where I come from, ladies are always in short supply."

"Erm…Lady Lovejoy mentioned you've been living in Texas. Is that part of America?"

Stephanie shook her head. "Texas is a sovereign republic

which borders the Gulf of Mexico. Unfortunately, I think Texas is going to be annexed to the United States as the twenty-eighth state this year. It's too bad, really. Texians are known to be independent."

"Did I hear an *I* in Texian?"

"Yes, you did." Stephanie giggled. "I think the I must stand for individualistic."

Juliet gestured toward the dining room, which had been set up as a buffet. "Would you care for a glass of punch?"

"Why not?"

As they crossed the hall, Stephanie giggled. "The countess has been trying to get me away from the billiards table for a half hour. I could tell she disapproved."

"Forgive me for saying so, but it's rather unusual for a young lady to mix with gentlemen in such an unguarded fashion."

"And I must rein myself in if I'm to catch a husband?" A sound of disgust. "I think I'd rather die than marry a man who won't let me have fun. Besides which, my brother and father were watching over me. I could hardly besmirch my reputation under their vigilant supervision."

As Juliet picked up a cut-crystal cup of cold punch, she stifled a smile. "I suppose not."

She'd never heard a girl give her opinions so decidedly, but she found Stephanie's rebellious streak somewhat refreshing. Even her gown was unusual. Although it was fashioned of snowy white silk, the beautiful dress made liberal use of insouciant cherry-red bows, as if it were thumbing its nose at convention. Juliet's prejudice against the Texian began to slip away.

"Your gown is exceedingly fetching, Miss Gryphon."

"Thank you. Almost as soon as we crossed the Atlantic, Papa insisted the three of us travel to Paris. He wanted me clothed in the latest fashions so I'd fit in with London society. I confess, however, behaving like a lady will be a challenge. I wasn't raised around stuffy, proper aristocrats who can't bear the idea of a woman shooting, riding astride, or playing billiards as well as they can."

Juliet nearly spilled her punch. "You ride astride?" The question came out with a bit of a squeak at the end. "If Lady Lovejoy ever heard as much, she'd likely faint dead away!"

Stephanie laughed at her shocked expression. "You're really quite proper, aren't you? I imagine the countess hopes you'll influence me for the better."

"Perhaps we might influence one another just a little bit. After all, I do admire your confidence very much."

"My brother, Cody, calls me arrogant, but he's only teasing. Besides which, I'm only confident on the outside. Inside, I'm as eager to be liked as anyone else."

"Your brother resembles Lord Gryphon a great deal."

"I'm told he does, but I've never met our cousin. Cody used to play with Zachary when they were very young, but he doesn't remember him with any particular fondness." Stephanie took a sip of punch and wrinkled her nose. "Too sweet! This would taste so much better with a splash or two of gin."

When Juliet gasped, Stephanie giggled. "I expect I'm not supposed to say things like that either."

"As a general rule, a lady should never express too much fondness for spirits."

"How very dull. Tell me, Miss Beaucroft, are you engaged?"

"No, not yet."

"Surely you must have prospects?"

Nothing—not even her growing regard for Stephanie—could induce Juliet to mention Augustus's name. Albeit unwittingly, before Kitty and Phillip's wedding, Juliet had let slip information about the courtship that had nearly ruined both their families. After that, she'd vowed never to be indiscreet about personal matters again.

"None at the moment." Juliet decided to change the subject.

"Let's circulate around the party and I'll introduce you to everyone I know. You've come into the Season quite late, so you haven't a moment to spare if you wish to find a husband."

"It's my father who's keen on the idea, not I. Nevertheless, I'm quite willing to make a new friend…as long as he's exceedingly handsome."

The two girls shared a merry laugh.

MISERY

Cody glanced up from his cards as his sister chatted with Lady Lovejoy and another young woman. He had only a frustratingly brief glimpse of the woman's face as she turned around, but her profile was lovely. In addition, her dainty figure was pleasing to the eye—especially from the back—and her lustrous dark golden hair reminded him pleasantly of a Palomino pony.

He addressed the older gentleman seated to his left. "Lord Ferndale, are you acquainted with that girl chatting with my sister and the countess?"

The three other occupants of the table, including his father, watched the ladies as they strolled from the room. Although Lord Ferndale opened his mouth to reply, the gentleman to Cody's right, Mr. Quincy, answered his question first.

"Miss Juliet Beaucroft." He smirked. "She's quite lovely, but you're too late."

"Too late?" Cody's eyebrows rose. "What do you mean?"

"Rumor has it that Lord Elbourne is exceedingly fond of her. I wouldn't be surprised if he makes her an offer quite soon."

Cody exchanged a surreptitious glance with his father. "Lord *Elbourne*, did you say?"

"Augustus Butler, the Earl of Elbourne and the future Marquess of Moregate."

"Yes…I've heard the name."

Lord Ferndale put his cards down and picked up the stub of his cigar. "Although it seems a bit lopsided in terms of rank, the match is inevitable, I think. After Elbourne's brother wed Miss Beaucroft's sister, he and Miss Beaucroft have been thrown together a great deal."

Lord Horatio frowned. "Miss Beaucroft seems a bit young to settle down, wouldn't you say? Another handsome lad may turn her head yet."

"He'd have to be exceptionally fortunate to woo her away from an earl." Ferndale folded his cards and put them face down on the table. "Gentlemen, I propose we take a short break, if you don't mind?"

"Of course." Quincy reached for his snifter. "I could use another splash of cognac, and a chance to stretch my legs."

Ferndale pushed his chair back. "Shall we say ten minutes?"

After the two men left, Cody gave his father a puzzled glance. "What's this about Miss Beaucroft? I thought you and Lord Moregate had exchanged letters quite recently to confirm Stephanie's engagement to Lord Elbourne?"

"Yes, but Moregate may not have convinced Lord Elbourne to agree to the match yet. I've no doubt he'll manage—despite any tender feelings the fellow may or may not harbor for Miss Beaucroft."

"Seems horribly unfair to Stephanie if the earl's in love with someone else. Perhaps you should reconsider? After all, there's always next Season for her to catch a husband."

"I promised your mother to have your sister marry an aristocrat, and I mean to keep my word."

"Yes, I know, but—"

"A union between Stephanie and the future Marquess of Moregate is the best chance for us to fulfill her wishes. In this case, the sentiments of the parties involved don't matter a whit."

Cody sighed. "Marriage is a messy business. I plan to avoid it."

"All the more reason to see your sister well settled, lad, and I expect you to do what you can to facilitate the process. Moregate is motivated to bring this marriage about, and the time to act is now."

JULIET PLAYED the part of hostess, introducing Stephanie to her acquaintances—both male and female. Since the girl was vivacious and charming, the task wasn't particularly difficult. In fact, Juliet found she was having a far better time than she'd anticipated.

At length, Stephanie's brother joined them. Again, Juliet was struck by his uncanny resemblance to his cousin, whose handsome visage and trim figure had made him the object of much female admiration...until his poor character had ruined his reputation. Cody's good looks were sure to set many pulses racing...as she could personally attest.

"Miss Beaucroft, have you met my brother, Cody?" Stephanie gave him a proud smile. "Cody, this is my newest, dearest friend, Miss Juliet Beaucroft."

"What a beautiful name." The man fixed Juliet with his dark brown eyes. "'Heaven is here, where Juliet lives.'" He sketched a graceful bow.

His accent was vastly different than his sister's, she noticed, and his quote brought a smile to her lips. Texians, it seemed, were not so far removed from society as to be wholly uneducated. "I see you know Shakespeare."

"Not personally, but I understand the man is reputed to be verbose. Are you acquainted with him?"

She gave him a sidelong glance. "We're intimate companions. He borrowed my name for his play, you see. The foolish author was going to call it *Romeo and Gertrude*, but I convinced him otherwise."

"Another burning mystery solved! The world is in your debt. *Romeo and Gertrude* simply doesn't have the same ring."

Stephanie shook her head. "You two are terribly silly, I must say. Cody, have any pretty ladies caught your eye tonight? Papa is sure to demand a full report."

"You know better than to ask."

Juliet's curiosity was aroused by the evasion, but Stephanie satisfied it almost immediately. "My brother is determined to return to Texas as soon as I'm settled, Miss Beaucroft."

"I own property there." He shrugged. "I left England when I was seven. Having spent most of my life in Texas, I've developed an affinity for wide open spaces."

"But your roots are English." Juliet smiled. "Perhaps your affection for England will reemerge, if you give it a chance."

Stephanie laughed. "That's exactly what I said! Perhaps between the two of us, we may yet change my brother's mind."

Although Juliet murmured an affirmative reply, she wasn't so sure she wished to change Cody's mind at all. Everything about the man, from his graceful movements to his witty conversation, appealed to her far too much for her liking. For the remainder of the evening, she tried to curb the physical sensations he aroused whenever he was near her. As attractive as he might be, his heart belonged to Texas and her heart belonged to Augustus…if the earl would finally bend his knee to propose.

∼

AFTER JULIET WAS ready for bed that night, she took a piece of stationery and wrote her future signature—Lady Elbourne—with a quill. She practiced various ways of making the looping L, from very simple to quite fancy. Kitty had become Lady Phillip Butler, which looked lovely on her correspondence, but once Juliet married Augustus, she'd outrank her sister. That wasn't why she wished to marry Augustus, she reminded herself, but it was a droll thought, particularly since Kitty had always come first in everything else.

Unbidden, Cody Gryphon's dangerously handsome face flashed into her mind's eye. He'd been flirting with her earlier, but perhaps that was his unbridled manner with every pretty girl. Nevertheless, if she hadn't already denied having a suitor to Stephanie, she would have mentioned her upcoming engagement to warn him off. Oh, well, it couldn't be too much longer before Augustus made it official, and then everyone would know she was off the market. She couldn't wait to write Kitty the news and see her reaction! Surely Christmas wouldn't be too soon for a wedding, would it? How lovely family get-togethers would be going forward, especially once children began to arrive. As she imagined it all, Juliet sighed with happiness. She was truly blessed.

AT BREAKFAST, Juliet ate quietly while her mother told her father all about the Ayscoghe soirée, from the array of refreshments to the guest list. Mr. Beaucroft made the proper responses here and there, but his attention was focused mainly on his food and his newspaper.

Finally, Mrs. Beaucroft's gaze rested on Juliet. "I noticed you made some new friends last night." She shuddered. "Mr. Gryphon certainly resembles that odious Lord Gryphon. I couldn't get past it."

At that, Mr. Beaucroft looked up. "Eh? What's this about Lord Gryphon? Surely he wasn't at the party. I'd heard the man isn't received anywhere any longer."

"No, Papa." Juliet explained the relationship between Cody Gryphon and his cousin. "Admittedly, the two gentlemen look alike, but Mr. Gryphon lacks Lord Gryphon's brittle and arrogant manner."

Her mother scoffed. "Certainly he exhibited no brittleness toward you. I couldn't help but notice you seemed to receive his attentions with pleasure."

"He was merely amiable and courteous, Mama. There was nothing untoward in his behavior whatsoever."

"Nevertheless, I'm glad Augustus wasn't there to take offense."

Mr. Beaucroft raised a skeptical eyebrow. "Furthermore, I can't imagine any relatives of Lord Gryphon could possess good character. It would be better for you to eschew his company, Juliet."

She frowned. "Since Lady Lovejoy asked me specifically to cultivate Miss Gryphon, I could scarcely treat her or her brother like pariahs."

"That's true, dearest." Mrs. Beaucroft gave her husband a look of resignation. "A request from the countess is akin to a summons from Her Majesty."

"Besides which, I enjoyed the company of the Gryphons very much. As soon as Augustus returns, we'll all be great friends, I'm sure. No misunderstandings could possibly ensue thereafter."

"I hope not." Mr. Beaucroft scowled. "You must do nothing to jeopardize your relationship with Augustus."

"I won't, Papa. I'm honored that Lady Lovejoy asked me to help Miss Gryphon. It's a shame the girl wasn't in London for the entire Season, when I could have done so much more. As it is, she'll likely have to wait until next year to meet someone eligible."

Mrs. Beaucroft radiated satisfaction. "Next year she'll be on her own, if a certain happy event takes place for you."

Although Juliet felt a blush creep across her face, she couldn't help but smile. "If that's the case, I'll use my lofty connections to secure her a husband as much as I'm able. Of course, we should take nothing for granted. I needn't remind you, Augustus hasn't yet proposed."

"If you can't take Augustus's devotion for granted, neither can you claim water is wet. Everyone expects your announcement any day." Mr. Beaucroft regarded Juliet fondly. "Your first Season has been quite successful, despite the handicap of your sister's unusual courtship and marriage. I wouldn't have predicted you would marry better than Kitty, but to have a countess in the family will be a triumph indeed."

"And future marchioness. I've said nothing about it to my friends, of course, but I'm looking forward to doing so with great anticipation." Mrs. Beaucroft gave an excited wiggle. "They'll be pea green with envy!"

Her family's happiness at her impending engagement gave Juliet untold satisfaction, but Augustus's title meant less to her than his affection. Had he been a mere gentleman, and not an earl, she still would have been honored to be his bride. She vowed to do whatever she could to make his life rich and rewarding. Nothing less would be sufficient for such a decent man and a good friend.

MIDMORNING, Juliet and her mother met in the library to pore over the remaining social engagements of the Season. Specifically, Juliet was looking for opportunities to include Stephanie wherever possible.

"I'll write a note inviting Miss Gryphon to go riding with me on Rotten Row tomorrow morning. We can talk about other outings then."

"Why don't you write a letter of thanks to Lady Ayscoghe, and we'll have a servant deliver both letters straightaway?"

"Excellent idea."

Juliet hastened over to the writing desk, and composed a note to Lady Ayscoghe in her best hand. Afterward, she began her letter to Stephanie, but before she'd written more than a few lines, a knock came at the front door of the townhouse.

Her mother glanced up from her embroidery hoop. "Who on earth could be calling at such an early hour?"

"Perhaps Miss Gryphon? Social etiquette may be vastly different in Texas."

When a deep male voice was heard in the entrance hall, Juliet wondered if Augustus had returned to London. She glanced at the drawing room door expectantly, but Watson failed to show the earl inside.

Mrs. Beaucroft shrugged and returned to her needlework. "It must have been someone to see your father."

Juliet finished her letter to Stephanie. Just as she'd sealed the envelope with wax and pressed it with the Beaucroft seal, the butler appeared in the doorway and cleared his throat.

"Forgive me for interrupting, but Mr. Beaucroft requests the company of Miss Beaucroft in his study. Lord Moregate has asked to speak with her."

"Lord Moregate?" Juliet frowned. "Is Lord Elbourne with him?"

"No, miss."

She exchanged a puzzled glance with her mother. Why would the marquess call on her father, and what further business did he have with *her*? On her way from the room, Juliet gave her letters to the butler.

"Watson, will you see that these messages are delivered by one of the servants?"

"Right away, Miss Beaucroft."

The Marquess of Moregate stood as Juliet entered her father's study. The older man was drawn and pale, and immediately, she feared the worst.

"Is Augustus all right, milord? Has anything happened to him?"

"He's perfectly well, I assure you. I'm sorry if I caused you any alarm in that regard. Still, I bring you no glad tidings, I'm afraid."

Mr. Beaucroft appeared to be unusually sober as he gestured toward a chair. "Please sit, Juliet, while Lord Moregate explains the nature of his visit."

She took a seat and waited patiently for someone to speak. What the marquess said next caught her so off guard, she thought she must not have heard him correctly.

"Miss Beaucroft, you cannot marry my son."

Speechless, she could only stare. Although Moregate proceeded to describe the financial difficulties which prohibited Augustus from marrying freely, she was only half attending. All she could hear was the sound of her future happiness being ground into a bloody pulp beneath his feet.

"I summoned Augustus home when I realized the extent of this unfolding disaster, but he refuses to listen to reason."

Tears began to leak from the corners of Juliet's eyes, which she didn't bother to hide or wipe away. Her predicament had coaxed a sheen of emotion into her father's eyes, too, and he rose from behind his desk to press a handkerchief into her hands.

"Augustus means to propose to you anyway, despite his obligations to his family." Moregate shook his head. "Please understand, Miss Beaucroft, under different circumstances we would have welcomed you to the family. Now, however, such a marriage can only mean the ruination of our estate."

"What are you asking me to do, Lord Moregate?" The calmness in Juliet's voice surprised her.

"Should Augustus insist on making you an offer, I'm begging you to refuse."

Her stomach contracted, and it was all she could do not to be sick on the oriental rug in her father's office.

Moregate continued. "Just this morning, I finished negotiating the terms of a marriage between Augustus and an heiress. Her father and I may have agreed financially, but the task remains to convince the two young parties involved that it's the proper course of action. Augustus refuses to cooperate, unfortunately, and we must help him see the virtues of the union. If you truly care for my son, Miss Beaucroft, you'll do what's right."

She blotted her eyes. "Which heiress is the subject of this agreement, Lord Moregate?"

"I'm told you met her at Lord and Lady Ayscoghe's soirée. Miss Stephanie Gryphon."

Was she in some sort of hideous nightmare, or was life playing a cruel joke? Her body went numb with shock, and blood seemed to be roaring in her ears. Stephanie Gryphon was destined to become Lady Elbourne, and she, Juliet, must encourage the match? It was too much to bear.

NOT CONTENT TO STAY INDOORS ON such a fine morning, Cody's sister convinced him to join her in an archery match after breakfast. He wasn't difficult to persuade, in fact, because he hoped to distract her from their father's absence. Although Stephanie had been told only that Lord Horatio was meeting someone for breakfast, Cody knew their father was hammering out financial details with the Marquess of Moregate, regarding her arranged marriage to Lord Elbourne.

The two siblings strolled out to a broad expanse of lawn where the target had been set onto a large easel. They tried to outdo one another in marksmanship, but to Cody's dismay, she managed to hit the bullseye more often than he did. After the first set, while they were retrieving their arrows, Stephanie gave him a shrewd glance.

"I don't wish to detract from my victory, but I can tell you're preoccupied this morning. Might your thoughts be straying to Miss Beaucroft, by any chance?"

"Of course not."

"She's a lovely girl, Cody. I hope you don't plan to trifle with her affections."

He pretended to take offense. "Why would you say such a thing?"

"Ever since we left Texas, you've been quite insistent about returning as soon as possible…no doubt to romance half the *señoritas* in the Republic. Since I wish to remain Miss Beaucroft's friend, I urge you to treat her with respect. She's almost like the sister I never had."

"That's absurd. How can you claim such intimacy after such a short acquaintance?"

"With some people, you just feel as if you've known them forever."

"I've never felt that way with anyone, most especially after only a few short hours."

"Hullo!" Lord Horatio appeared on the patio and gestured for them to join him.

"It appears Father has something to share," Cody said.

"Do you suppose he found a residence to purchase? Although Lady Lovejoy has been most kind and hospitable, I don't wish to impose on her much longer."

Cody feigned ignorance of his father's activities. "It does no good to speculate."

He put his bow and arrows down and escorted his sister

back to the house. As soon as they stepped through the patio doors, the butler appeared to present Stephanie with a letter. "This just arrived for you, Miss Gryphon. And Lord Horatio asked me to say he's awaiting your company and that of Mr. Gryphon in the library."

Cody nodded. "Thank you, Yeats."

Stephanie's eyebrows rose when she saw the return address on the envelope. "Oh, I've had a letter from Miss Beaucroft. I can't wait to read it!"

Inwardly, Cody grimaced. If Juliet had heard about the proposed union between Lord Elbourne and his sister, she may have written her an angry, poisonous letter. If so, Stephanie would learn about the arrangement in the worst possible fashion. As his sister broke the wax seal on the envelope, he touched her hand.

"Why don't you read your letter after we speak with Father? He seemed to have something important to say."

"How could you tell? We were several hundred feet apart."

"Er…it was the purposeful set of his head."

She peered at him. "Really? I didn't realize you were that observant."

He swept his arm toward the library doors. "After you."

As soon as Cody entered the room, he could tell from his father's smile of satisfaction that the meeting with Lord Moregate had gone well. Even more telling was the exuberant kiss he deposited on Stephanie's cheek.

"You are the most fortunate of women." He laughed. "Cody, we're in the presence of a future countess, Lady Elbourne."

If Horatio expected his daughter to jump up and down with glee, he was mistaken. Instead, she stepped backward with a wary expression.

"What are you talking of, Papa? I've never even met Lord Elbourne."

"The young earl is in want of a wife. I've proposed you and my offer has been accepted. You're to be wed no later than Christmas, or as soon as the arrangements can be made." He beamed. "I couldn't be more proud!"

Stephanie quivered with outrage. "Are you out of your senses, Papa? These are modern times, and you can't just marry off your daughter to an earl, sight unseen. I refuse!"

Cody bit the inside of his cheek and gazed at the ceiling. He'd cautioned his father to wait until after Stephanie and Lord Elbourne had been introduced before suggesting the match, but the bull-headed man had insisted she'd be thrilled at the notion of marrying an earl.

His sister glared. "What do you have to say about this travesty, Cody?"

He frowned. "Er...well, it seems harsh to force you into a marriage you don't want." Over Stephanie's head, his father shot him a pained glance. "On the other hand, considering Lord Elbourne's rank, it would be foolish to refuse the match without ever having met the fellow."

"What? Cody, you can't seriously approve of this!"

He shrugged. "It's not for me to approve or disapprove. Nevertheless, I want you to be happy."

She threw her arms around him as if he were a life preserver. "I knew I could count on you."

"Yes, of course. Um...I understand Lord Elbourne has a reputation for impeccable character."

Horatio nodded. "Yes, that's so. Nobody has anything ill to say of him."

Stephanie grimaced. "He sounds completely horrible!"

Cody laughed. "How could you reach that odd conclusion?"

"Nobody has anything ill to say about chamber pots either, but nobody wants to see them in plain view!"

Horatio made a sound of disgust. "Really, Stephanie, must

you be so vulgar? We're not in Texas any longer, and I expect you to comport yourself like a lady."

Dark clouds were brewing over Stephanie's head, and Cody sought to head things off before the storm broke. "I encourage you to keep an open mind. Mother expressed a desire for you to marry nobility and have children on English soil."

"She did?"

"Indeed, it was always her intention you should return to England, to marry well," Horatio said.

A flicker of doubt crossed her face. "Really?"

Cody sensed a crack in her armor. "Furthermore, did you know Lord Elbourne's brother is married to Miss Beaucroft's sister? If you marry the earl, you and Miss Beaucroft would be extended family."

"Be that as it may, I know nothing about him. What if he's hideous, with tufts of nose hair, a pot belly, wrinkled earlobes, and has the disposition of a rattlesnake?"

Horatio's chuckle at the unflattering description was cut short by Stephanie's scowl. "Er...I've not met Lord Elbourne, but his father is a particular acquaintance of mine from my days at Oxford. Moregate has retained his youthful handsome swagger, and undoubtedly Augustus is the same way."

"Augustus? What sort of stupid name is that?"

"The name is of very noble origin, actually," Horatio said. "The founder of the Roman Empire went by that name."

Stephanie rolled her eyes. "The question was rhetorical, Papa."

Cody tried an appeal to his sister's reasonable nature. "Let's not argue any further until we've had a chance to get acquainted with Lord Elbourne. If he's not a troll, we can proceed accordingly."

His father gave an emphatic nod. "A level-headed suggestion if ever I heard one."

Seemingly despite herself, Stephanie began to giggle. "A troll?"

"A troll has tufts of nose hair, a pot belly, and wrinkled earlobes, does he not? You should have added dragging knuckles and curly tusks to the list of grotesqueries…although perhaps that's an ogre."

"You're setting the bar rather low, Cody. If Lord Elbourne looks anything like a troll or an ogre, *you* can marry him!"

"I'm just teasing you. I've every confidence my future brother-in-law will be exceedingly amiable, as handsome as a god, and flowing with the milk of human kindness."

She gave him a sidelong glance. "Now the bar is set too high. At a minimum, I must be able to tolerate the man for more than ten minutes at a time. We'll see about the rest."

Cody embraced her. "That's the spirit."

Horatio breathed a sigh of relief. "We've been invited to Lord and Lady Ferndale's ball Friday evening. We'll meet Lord Elbourne then."

"I hope Miss Beaucroft will be there. Perhaps she mentioned it in her letter." Stephanie retrieved the letter from her pocket and skimmed the contents. "Ah! She's invited me to ride with her tomorrow morning. I'll write her back immediately to accept."

After she hastened from the room, Cody and his father exchanged a grim glance.

"Well done, lad. You managed to diffuse the situation admirably."

"We're not in the clear yet. Stephanie has developed an attachment to Miss Beaucroft, and values her opinion. If the girl warns Stephanie away from Lord Elbourne out of spite, it would be a disaster."

"Good point, that." Horatio pondered a moment. "When they go riding together tomorrow, you must accompany the two of them as chaperone. We can't afford to let Miss Beaucroft ruin what has begun in such a promising fashion."

"For Mother's sake, I'll do whatever I can to make sure the wedding takes place." Cody's eyebrows drew together. "I do hope Lord Elbourne is deserving of Stephanie."

"I have every confidence he is."

SMUDGE

*J*uliet curled up on her bed all morning, spiritless. Tea was brought, but merely sat on her bedside table, untouched. Mr. Beaucroft had offered to summon a physician, but she'd declined that, too. After all, there were no cures for disappointment.

Her mother had taken the news even worse than *she* had, if the volume of her protests was to be the measure. Thank heavens Lord Moregate had departed long before or he would have received an earful, too. Even behind closed doors, she could hear her mother berating her father for acceding to the marquess's wishes.

"*Everyone* expects Juliet to become engaged to Augustus, Gaylord! If he throws her over now, she'll be humiliated beyond measure!"

"Since he must marry someone else, there's nothing to be done about it. Surely by next Season, the gossips will have some other scandal to salivate over."

"Augustus has jilted our daughter and you don't seem to care a whit!"

"He's done no such thing. Besides which, would you rather

see the Butler family fall into ruin? Juliet is only eighteen, dearest. She has plenty of time to find a husband."

"You seem to think aristocrats with titles grow on trees! Juliet hasn't got Kitty's dramatic good looks to rely on, or her vivacity. Augustus might be her last chance to marry."

"Nonsense. You've always been partial to Kitty's appearance, perhaps, but Juliet's an extraordinarily pretty girl, by any measure. Furthermore, I've always admired her wit!"

"Augustus ought to be ashamed of what he's doing to our girl. She'll be an object of pity hereinafter and end up on the shelf."

Although Juliet appreciated her father's loyalty, she squeezed a pillow around her head to muffle her mother's insults. It was dreadfully unfair to compare her to her sister in terms of looks. Kitty was more beautiful than everyone, and besides which, she was married now. Perhaps her mother was just upset, but the comments hurt nevertheless. Even worse was the notion that Juliet would soon be seen as an object of pity and possibly even ridicule.

Indeed, she felt good and sorry for herself. She'd planned on becoming a countess, the mistress of a grand estate, with an extensive household to manage. Her engagement would have been the unparalleled coup of the Season, astonishing everyone who'd thought her less pretty and desirable than her sister. Now, her dreams were in ashes.

Certainly she could still choose to accept Augustus's proposal of marriage, should he make her an offer. She could happily live in reduced circumstances as long as she had Augustus by her side...but would she enjoy her own selfish pleasure, knowing it had been secured at a horrendous cost to him and his family? On the other hand, how would she feel watching another woman take her place?

With no appetite and no desire to speak with anyone, Juliet refused lunch. Midafternoon, the maid brought her another cup of hot tea to replace the one that had grown cold, as well as a few biscuits. The maid also delivered a message from Stephanie which, Juliet presumed, was an answer to her invitation earlier that morning. She forced herself to sit up and drink the hot, bracing beverage. Thus fortified, she read Stephanie's letter:

Dear Miss Beaucroft,

I accept with pleasure your invitation to ride tomorrow morning, and I promise not to ride astride! Also, I intend to ask your opinion on a matter of great importance. We've only just met, but I suspect your advice will be both unbiased and trustworthy. Until tomorrow, then.

Very Truly Yours,

Stephanie

P.S. Cody insists on accompanying us as a chaperone. I hope you don't mind.

The ink on the letter smeared as Juliet's tears fell anew. Feeling as she did, could her advice to Stephanie possibly be considered unbiased and trustworthy? For Augustus's sake, she prayed she was up to the task.

Nevertheless, since the Butlers' financial situation was a closely-guarded secret, she suspected her mother was right on one point at least: everyone would assume her inadequacies were to blame for losing Augustus. Juliet Beaucroft would forevermore be viewed as undesirable and pitiable. How could she hold her head up in society if people were snickering at her behind their hands? Since few men wished to court ladies passed over by other men, she'd be on the shelf after her first Season.

As she'd learned full well from Kitty, the use of a ruse could be dangerous and foolhardy—but she felt she had no choice. Therefore, before Augustus publicly threw her over, she must appear to throw him over first. How could she possibly manage it?

∼

WHEN CODY and his sister joined Juliet on Rotten Row before breakfast the following morning, he was shocked to see how pale and drawn she was. In addition, the skin around Juliet's eyes was puffy and pink, as if she'd been crying all night. Obviously she'd been told her union with Lord Elbourne was not to be. Something in his gut twisted at the evidence of her suffering, but he hardened his heart. His job was to make sure Juliet said nothing to prevent his sister from marrying the earl. He owed his allegiance to his mother's memory, not to a girl he barely knew. Surely, the young woman's disappointment would soon pass.

Cody tipped his hat. "Good morning, Miss Beaucroft. I'm delighted to see you again."

A ghost of a smile reached her lips, but not her eyes. "Good morning."

He sought to lift her spirits. "I enjoyed our conversation immensely at the Ayscoghe soirée. In fact, I can't remember when I've passed such a pleasant evening."

"You're too kind, Mr. Gryphon."

"I hope you're free tonight for dinner," Stephanie said. "Lady Lovejoy is sending you a written note by messenger, but she asked me to invite you to an intimate gathering of close friends."

"An intimate gathering for fifty, I daresay." Juliet's laugh seemed forced. "Nevertheless, I'm sure I'd love to attend."

Stephanie peered at her. "Are you ill? You look as if you didn't sleep a wink!"

"Thank you, but I'm perfectly well. It's quite silly, really, but I heard some bad news about a family pet last night. The caretaker at our country home wrote to say the dog ran off. I couldn't sleep for worry."

"Oh, no! I'm so terribly sorry. We had to give our dog to another family before we left Texas. I never cried so hard as when I said good-bye to Star. What's the name of your dog?"

If Cody had been in any doubt before, a long moment of hesitation convinced him of Juliet's dissembling.

"Er…Hamlet. Shall we ride?"

The trio urged their mounts onto the wide, sandy track known as Rotten Row, with Juliet positioned in between the two siblings. To Cody's surprise, a great many riders populated the path.

"I didn't realize Hyde Park would be so popular this early in the day."

Juliet's lips curved in another all-too-brief smile. "Oh, yes. Many a romance is begun or encouraged on horseback. If you're in town next April, you'll scarcely be able to trot your horse on Rotten Row. It's always quite crowded with hopefuls at the beginning of the Season."

Stephanie gave her a sidelong glance. "As much as I'd like to gallop, let's keep to a walk for a little while. As I wrote in my letter, I've something to confide. Truly, I hope you don't think me too forward in asking your opinion about Lord Elbourne?"

Juliet looked neither right nor left. "Ah, dear Augustus. What would you like to know?"

"Is he handsome?"

"I think him so. He hasn't the flashy good looks that the rakish set possess, I'll grant you. Instead, I would describe him as comfortable and steady, like a beautiful sunrise."

Stephanie's eyebrows rose. "What a lovely description! I confess you intrigue me…despite my prejudice to the contrary. You see, his father and mine are set on arranging a match."

"You have my most sincere congratulations, Miss Gryphon."

"Do call me Stephanie. I hope you don't think it's too soon for Christian names?"

"Not at all." Juliet smiled. "In my opinion, Augustus is a husband worth fighting for. To have an arranged marriage with him is good fortune beyond measure."

Cody was flabbergasted. If he'd expected Juliet's response to be dripping with bile or calculated to wound in retribution for her loss, he was greatly mistaken. Her ability to praise Lord Elbourne under the circumstances, and to encourage Stephanie's interest in him, indicated an unusual strength of character. His respect for Juliet soared—even as a modicum of jealousy toward the earl took root.

Stephanie cleared her throat. "Tell me more. What are Lord Elbourne's pursuits? How does he spend his days?"

He paid rapt attention to Juliet's response, wondering what amazing qualities the earl possessed to have captivated her so completely. She mentioned a few of his favorite books, a beloved collection of butterflies, and the fact he liked to sketch.

Stephanie wrinkled her nose. "Forgive me, but he sounds a trifle sedate."

Juliet finally laughed. "Perhaps Augustus needs a woman like you to spark his sense of adventure." Her merriment faded. "Now that I think on it, I daresay it wouldn't be beneficial for him to marry someone with a personality too similar to his own."

Cody nodded. "A sage observation, I warrant. There can be no compromise in matters of character, of course. Beyond that, however, I suspect relationships between persons of opposite temperament are often the most satisfying."

Stephanie leaned forward to gape at him. "I'm all astonishment, Cody. I'd no idea you'd ever thought much about matters of compatibility. You've perfected the means of escape from every pretty girl who ever crooked a finger in your direction."

When Juliet turned her head to gaze at him, he felt his cheekbones flare into a heated blush and he sought to defend himself.

"Nonsense, Stephanie. You'll have Miss Beaucroft thinking I'm a rake."

"If she doesn't think it now, I must certainly warn her off. Juliet, you mustn't take my brother seriously at all."

"I wouldn't dream of it."

The murmured reply rankled Cody for some reason. So Juliet wouldn't dream of taking him seriously? Aggrieved, he threw his shoulders back and lifted his chin. Perhaps he didn't measure up to the lofty standards of the glorious and superlative Lord Elbourne, but no woman had ever complained about his company before. Furthermore, he vowed to chastise his sister in private for her ill-considered jibe. The likelihood of an arranged marriage might set her nerves on edge, but she oughtn't take her disgruntlement out on him. He only wanted to see her happy, and she might want to reciprocate his efforts on her behalf. In the next moment, he wondered why such a bizarre thought had entered his mind. Juliet, though admittedly pretty and sweet, wasn't the key to his future happiness.

He gestured toward the path ahead. "Shall we pick up the pace? At this rate we won't finish our ride until lunch."

THE BOOK in Juliet's lap failed to capture her interest overmuch, but then nothing seemed to give her genuine pleasure that afternoon. Although her mother tried to tempt her with a trip to the milliner's, she'd declined the jaunt in favor of reading Jane Austen in her bedchamber. If only her life was a romance novel, it would all work out beautifully in the end. She used Lady Lovejoy's recently-arrived dinner invitation as a bookmark and stared out the window instead.

Her ride with the Gryphon siblings that morning had actually helped elevate her mood for a short while, although the exercise had been almost dreamlike. Never before had she been so torn about anyone as she was about Stephanie. Juliet wished to dislike her romantic rival, but she couldn't think of anything remotely unpleasant about the girl. If Stephanie ever hurt

Augustus, however, Juliet didn't think she could bear to be in the same room with her.

Cody's comment about paradoxical relationships often turning out to be the most satisfying had been quite thought-provoking. Although she'd let his observation go unremarked upon that morning, she'd since been struck by how insightful it was. The man was an unexpected philosopher, it seemed, as well as a prime example of male beauty. Perhaps it was unfair to be prejudiced against him, but the man's handsome face and trim figure made it easy for Juliet to believe he could play the flirt. Her admiration of his looks reminded her unpleasantly of her former admiration of Lord Gryphon. She'd hadn't known of the viscount's bad character at the time, of course. When she learned he'd tried to take advantage of Kitty, however, she'd been ashamed of seeing anything handsome about him at all. Since Stephanie had said her brother was a scoundrel, she'd redouble her efforts to inure herself to his charms. Forewarned was forearmed, as the saying went.

The notion of physical attraction had been in her thoughts a great deal as well. The way she'd felt when she'd first seen Augustus had been vastly different from her first view of Cody. Augustus had pleased her eye much the way she might admire a beautiful statue or a lovely landscape. With Cody, however, she'd felt a tug at her core, almost as if she were hungry. There was no doubt in her mind that she cared for Augustus, and would have made him a good wife. But she suspected her puzzling attraction to Cody Gryphon meant she wasn't passionately in love with Augustus the way Kitty adored Philip, or Prudence cherished her husband, Frederick. Furthermore, she and Augustus had passed a great deal of time together, but they'd never exchanged a kiss. When Juliet closed her eyes and allowed herself to imagine what it would be like to kiss Cody, her heart began to race and warmth spread through her veins. In the next moment, she pushed the feelings from her mind.

Once Stephanie was married, Cody would return to Texas, and her inconvenient physical attraction to him would fade away.

Until then, however, he could play a central role in her ruse.

THE DINNER at Lady Lovejoy's house—at which over three dozen guests were in attendance—was held in two sitting rooms linked together with double doors. Despite the large number of people, the party did have a sense of intimacy due to the relatively cozy size of the sitting rooms. To Juliet's annoyance, Cody was seated in the other room, so she had no opportunity to catch his eye.

After dinner, the ladies gathered in the drawing room for conversation and waited for the gentlemen to finish with their cigars and brandy. Juliet sought out the company of Mrs. Wormwood, whom she determined to be the most notorious gossipmonger in the party. As soon as the masculine contingent appeared, someone suggested a game of charades. In the mad scramble to arrange the furniture to create a stage, Juliet located Cody and murmured her request.

"I need your assistance with a personal matter, Mr. Gryphon. Will you join me in the library in a few minutes?"

He seemed taken aback. "Well…certainly. I'll be along directly."

With the sound of revelry at her back, Juliet slipped from the room and hastened down the hall. She stepped into the library and checked behind the drapery to make sure no prying ears or eyes could overhear the scene about to unfold. Once she'd satisfied herself the room was unoccupied, she positioned herself next to the fireplace to wait for Cody to arrive. In the very last moment, she remembered to adjust the neckline of her bodice as low as possible. After all, her request would fall on deaf ears if the gentleman found her repulsive.

Very shortly thereafter, Cody entered the room and shut the door behind him. "How may I help you, Miss Beaucroft?"

"Thank you for agreeing to speak with me."

Cody looked dashing and sophisticated in his elegantly tailored clothes, and Juliet was seized with an attack of nerves. Nevertheless, she cleared her throat and gave him a direct glance meant to convey a businesslike demeanor rather than one of coquetry.

"I'd like you to ruin me." Despite her best intentions, her words were immediately followed by a blush. Why couldn't she be more dispassionate?

His eyebrows rose. "What?"

"Just a little ruination, mind you. Nothing that can't be hushed up in a few months or so."

"I'm sorry, but I'm not understanding you at all."

"You're aware, of course, of the arrangement between Lord Moregate and your father regarding Stephanie and Lord Elbourne."

"Yes. My father is quite keen on the subject."

"What you don't know is that Augustus has been widely expected to propose to me."

"Actually, I'd heard rumors to that effect."

Juliet's eyes widened. "I hope Stephanie hasn't heard those rumors!"

"Not of which I'm aware."

A sigh of relief. "Good."

"I'm sorry for any injury this arrangement has done to you. I can tell you're quite partial to Lord Elbourne."

"I *am* partial to Augustus, and would have accepted his proposal if he'd asked. But after a careful examination of my feelings, I can truly say I'm not in love with him."

"You're not?" His eyebrows drew together. "If your feelings aren't injured, then what's this about?"

"Once society learns Augustus has thrown me off, I'll

become an object of ridicule. I mean to publicly throw him off before anyone hears about his engagement to Stephanie. For that, I need you to ruin me…ever so slightly."

He looked at her askance. "Won't your reputation be forevermore tarnished?"

"I'd rather be a little tarnished than humiliated, Mr. Gryphon. An earl is about to pass me over for another woman. Do you really think my prospects will be improved by such a spectacular rejection?" She averted her eyes. "If I'm to be ruined anyway, I'd rather choose the method."

"Have you no thought to *my* reputation?"

She waved her hands, dismissively. "Stephanie says you're a rake, doesn't she? Therefore, nobody will think less of you than they already do now. Amongst your male acquaintances, I daresay the rumor of a passing indiscretion would be well received. Besides which, you're leaving for Texas before too long, so what does your reputation matter?"

"Of course." He folded his arms over his chest. "For the sake of curiosity, what sort of ruination did you have in mind? After all, we are here alone in the library together. To some members of society, such intimate contact is scandalous."

"I've a reputation for being beyond reproach, I'm afraid, so you and I must push the boundaries a bit farther than a minor indiscretion."

"I'm open to suggestions. What do you propose?"

Now that the ruination had become less theoretical, Juliet became increasingly nervous. Despite that, she'd gone too far to back out now.

"Perhaps if I, um, sat in your lap? Before dinner, I asked Mrs. Wormwood to meet me in the library at nine o'clock."

"Mrs. Wormwood, did you say?"

"Yes. She should be here any moment to be a witness to our ruse. When she opens the library door, I'll jump up in a guilty fashion that will condemn our behavior."

Cody cocked his head. "She'll be here any moment, will she?" He sank down into a sturdy chair. "In that case, I'm ready when you are."

Juliet swallowed hard as she lowered herself gingerly sideways across his legs. "I'm not crushing you, am I?"

"I'm quite comfortable, thank you."

"Good." She sat there for several seconds, her spine ramrod straight. "As I said before, Mrs. Wormwood should be along directly. She's an awful gossip."

"Forgive me, but I don't think merely sitting on my lap goes far enough. Given your stature as a girl beyond reproach, I believe a more active participation is required to get the result you seek."

She felt her cheeks glowing even more. A more *active participation*, as he put it, wasn't anything she'd contemplated.

"I hadn't…well, that is to say, I-I'm not sure if I could…" She trailed off, nonplussed.

"Put your arms around my neck at least, and relax your posture somewhat. You don't appear to be enjoying yourself at all."

She bit her lower lip. "You don't mind?"

"Not in the least. It's for a good cause."

"All right." She rested her arms on his shoulders. "Is this what you mean?"

"Only if you want to be viewed as my maiden aunt." He reached up to reposition her arms, forcing her to drape her body against his. Then he put his hands under her legs and pulled her even closer. "That's much better, wouldn't you agree?"

"Mr. Gryphon!"

"Forgive me, but you want this to look authentic, don't you? Trust me, Miss Beaucroft. After all, if I'm a rake, I must be an expert in scandalous behavior, mustn't I?"

"I suppose so." She took a deep breath, blew it out slowly, and gave him a smile. "I look more relaxed now, don't I?"

"A little. Only...when Mrs. Wormwood walks in, you and I should be kissing."

Juliet stiffened. "Is that really necessary?"

"Oh, yes, if you truly want to smudge your reputation." His gaze fell to her mouth. "Shall we practice?"

She bent her head forward and brushed her lips against his so lightly that she wasn't even certain she'd made contact. His hands cupped her face and coaxed her forward. When his lips claimed hers, this time she felt it from the top of her head to the tips of her toes.

"That's it," he murmured.

"Are you sure it looks natural? I've never kissed anyone before."

"Oh, yes. I assure you, we're very authentic."

Several more delectable kisses went by before Juliet began to suspect something was wrong. "It must be past nine o'clock by now. I wonder where Mrs. Wormwood is?"

The tip of Cody's tongue probed hers for a few moments before he responded. "She went home."

Juliet pulled back. "You're joking."

"Mrs. Wormwood took her leave just before I came to meet you. I overheard her say she'd developed a dreadful headache."

She scrambled off his lap and glared at him. "So you knew she wasn't coming all along?"

"Yes, but I wasn't altogether sure nobody else would interrupt us...except that everyone is playing charades at the moment and I rather doubted it." He grinned as he got to his feet. "Would you like to practice a little more?"

UNEXPECTED ENCOUNTERS

*J*uliet wasn't usually given to flashes of anger, but her hand seemed to act of its own accord. Before she thought twice, she slapped him full across the face.

"You despicable cad!"

Despite the physical rebuke, Cody's grin barely slipped. Past furious, she used both hands to shove him backward. He lost his balance and ended up sitting in the chair once more, none too gracefully.

"Come now, Miss Beaucroft! You enlisted my cooperation in a ruse. If I'm a cad, what does that make you? Furthermore, despite my sister's characterization to the contrary, I'm not a rake."

"What?"

"Stephanie has always been protective of her elder brother and routinely tries to ward off anyone I might find remotely attractive."

"But Stephanie hasn't a duplicitous bone in her body!"

"Rest assured, it's done quite unconsciously on her part."

"I don't believe you."

"What's more, you had no compunction about risking *my* reputation just to allay theoretical concerns about what a group of harpies might say about you. To my way of thinking, you got what you deserve."

Although Juliet was angry at Cody for making a fool of her, she couldn't deny the truth of his assertions. Her dignity in shreds, she sought to extricate herself from the situation as graciously as possible. She smoothed her gown and lifted her chin.

"Forgive me for imposing on you, Mr. Gryphon. We shan't speak of this again."

"Don't apologize completely. I confess, I rather enjoyed myself."

Her eyes narrowed at his impertinent remark, but there was nothing more to say. She wrenched open the library door and fled down the hall toward to the drawing room. Since everyone's attention was focused on the charade participants, she had no trouble slipping through the doors and joining the onlookers in the back.

As Juliet pretended to watch the game, she felt as if she were the most foolish girl ever born. What must Cody think of her? When he slipped into the room a few minutes later, she refused to glance in his direction. She would pretend—as much as she was able—that nothing had occurred between them, despite the fact that she'd enjoyed his kisses more than she could have imagined in her wildest daydreams.

To Cody's amusement, Juliet was seemingly riveted on the game of charades and was actively ignoring him as much as a human being could ignore anything. He could scarcely blame her, really. When she'd made her absurd suggestion, he should have flatly refused to participate at the outset. Instead, he'd been curious just how far she meant to take her ruse. Maybe, if truth be told, he *had* acted the cad, but he was only human after all. Once she'd sat in his lap, he would have said anything to taste her sweet lips.

As the charades went on, amidst much laughter and frivolity, his eyes kept returning to Juliet's profile. A slight frown creased her brow, and it pained him to realize he was the cause of it. With a sigh, he folded his arms across his chest and wished she would return his gaze. Certainly, a few stolen kisses weren't worth the loss of her regard forever. On the other hand, hadn't she been all too willing to toss his reputation aside to save her own skin? Of course, he could probably hold his breath and turn the color of a plum before she'd ever apologize for it—or for calling him a rake. Asking his forgiveness for imposing on him wasn't the same thing whatsoever, especially since she'd been trying to extricate herself from an awkward situation.

Despite his grievance, Juliet's confession regarding her platonic feelings for the earl pleased him—admittedly not just on Stephanie's behalf. When they'd been alone together in the library, her revelation had practically aroused a raging beast within him. As his blood stirred at the memory, he pushed the recollection aside. With a Herculean effort, he averted his eyes from Juliet's creamy complexion and lustrous hair and stared at the nearby decorative brass coal hod instead. Any train of thought which led in her direction would come to naught. No woman, no matter how exquisitely lovely, or arrestingly intelligent, would change his plans for the future. As soon as his sister was wed, he meant to set sail from England and never look back, whatever temptations might remain on English soil.

Augustus spent most of the journey to London deep in thought. He'd spent several days examining the financial condition of the estate and speaking with Mr. Kelly about his plans going forward. To his disappointment, he discovered his father hadn't overstated the problem. Kelly had proposed quickly and quietly putting the worst-performing properties up for sale, which Augustus heartily endorsed. Unfortunately, transactions of that magnitude would take time he didn't have.

He was not altogether convinced that marriage to Juliet would lead to financial ruin. Nevertheless, drastic and potentially mortifying economies would be necessary. With Kelly's help, he'd drawn up a list of austerity measures to present to his father, who was the only one legally entitled to act on it. In Augustus's opinion, expecting him and Juliet to bear the brunt of this calamity was deeply unfair. Therefore, he was determined to marry where his heart led him, and nowhere else—despite the consequences. Perhaps his actions could be termed reckless and selfish, but he didn't care.

At the edges of his mind, however, persistent doubts lingered. It would be difficult to watch his father leave Meadow's End and suffer a loss of prestige, but inconceivable to force his dear mother to do the same. Furthermore, if his father was obliged to sell the note on Grovebrook to raise funds, Philip would have absolutely no leeway in making payments to the new creditor. Since his younger brother had worked so hard to purchase the property, it would grieve Augustus very much if he and Kitty lost it due to a lackluster quarter.

By the time his train reached London, Augustus had changed his mind so often, his head ached. Ultimately, however, he absolutely decided in favor of Juliet. She had a right to know his financial situation before she accepted him, however, so he would tell her without embellishment or obfuscation. They would face the consequences together, as the future Lord and Lady Elbourne.

Outside the rail station, he hailed a cab to take him to the residence his father had recently purchased. He had been accustomed to staying with his cousin, Lady Trestlebury, whenever he came to town. Unfortunately, Lord Trestlebury had barred any of the Butlers from his home. Ever since Philip assisted Lord Trestlebury's daughter, Prudence, with her elopement, there had been a deep schism in the family. Although the new Mayfair residence was befitting the stature of the Butler family, Augustus now bitterly regretted the expenditure. No doubt the residence—named The Aerie—would have to be sold before any of them could really enjoy it.

He ate a late lunch in the dining room of his gentlemen's club, but had little appetite. Ordinarily, a man on the cusp of proposing would feel apprehension as a matter of course. In his case, however, the prospect was far less appealing than usual due to his looming financial disaster. Juliet would undoubtedly have some encouragement to offer. Just being near her would steady his nerves. He slipped his hand into his coat pocket to make sure the engagement ring was there. The cool circle of gold and opals had been his grandmother's favorite ring. When he was quite young, he used to lean on her knee, the better to admire the fiery inset stones. Now it was time to present the heirloom to his future bride.

After changing his shirt for a fresh one, Augustus took a cab to the Beaucroft's Belgravia residence. With the clip-clop of horse's hooves ringing in his ears, he rehearsed exactly what he was going to say until he had it down perfectly. All that remained was for him to deliver his proposal and wait for Juliet's answer.

JULIET SPENT the day in her bedroom, confused. She knew she was out of her senses, but she couldn't seem to marshal her thoughts. No matter how much she tried lose herself in a book or in writing a letter, the memory of Cody's kisses distracted her so much she couldn't concentrate at all. The remainder of the party had consisted of her avoiding the man and counting the seconds until she could take her leave.

Midafternoon, a tap came at Juliet's door, and a maid appeared. "Miss Beaucroft, Lord Elbourne has come to call."

An incomprehensible mixture of pleasure and dread accompanied the announcement.

"Has he?"

"I wouldn't have disturbed you, but neither Mr. nor Mrs. Beaucroft are at home. Shall I send him away?"

"No." She closed her book and rose to her feet. "I'll be down momentarily, Alice."

After the maid left, Juliet hastened to the mirror to smooth her hair and to dab a moistened handkerchief on the skin underneath her eyes. She sighed as she examined her reflection. Her appearance was certainly less than perfect, but it would have to suffice.

When she entered the drawing room, her brother-in-law was pacing in the center of the room, clearly agitated.

"Augustus, I'm so glad to see you."

She crossed to him and gave his hands a squeeze. His expression was strained, and dark shadows encircled his eyes. All things considered, she decided against feigning ignorance of his situation. That much of his burden she could shoulder.

"Your papa came to see us the other day, and told us of your difficulties. I'm sorry for your troubles."

His eyebrows drew together and a flash of anger animated his face. "He'd no right to come here without conferring with me first!"

"Perhaps not, but I'm glad he did, You need supportive friends around you now, more than ever."

"Well...I'm relieved that you know." He frowned. "I came to ask you something, Juliet, but I—" he was obliged to take a deep breath before he could continue "—I came to ask you to marry me…but I can't."

Bittersweet joy exploded in Juliet's chest. "Oh, thank heavens. I'm so glad."

"What?"

"Knowing you as I do, I couldn't conceive of any circumstance in which you'd turn your back on your family. No matter what the difficulty, you've always been a man of the highest character, Augustus. I can't tell you how happy I am not to be your downfall."

He gazed at her face in wonderment for several seconds. "You're extraordinary."

"Not really. I admit I was disappointed to learn I would never become your wife, but now I see it as a blessing in disguise. You and I are so much alike, I think we're better off as friends. If you examine your feelings for me carefully, I suspect you'll come to the same conclusion."

"Better friends than lovers?"

"Exactly."

"Perhaps you're right." He enfolded her in his arms. "I do love you, Juliet."

"As I love you, Augustus. Never forget, you'll always be my dearest confidant."

When he stepped back, his eyes were moist. "I must marry someone else, and quite soon."

"Yes, I know. As it happens, I've met Miss Stephanie Gryphon and approve of her without reservation. She and her family are staying with Lady Lovejoy, and the countess asked me to befriend her. I like her very much."

"You do?" He sighed. "I suppose that's something in her favor."

"Give Stephanie a chance, Augustus, for her sake as well as your own. I wouldn't be at all surprised if you fall in love with her."

"I can't imagine such a thing, but I'll try."

The earl kissed her on the cheek, retrieved his hat and left the house. Juliet was relieved that she and Augustus had let each other go more easily than she'd anticipated, but she wasn't looking forward to the aftermath. His public courtship and subsequent engagement to Stephanie Gryphon were sure to provoke a barrage of impertinent and uncharitable remarks. Her ability to catch a husband would be brought into question, and there was nothing to be done about it except wait until next Season and hope memories would fade.

Kitty's image smiled down at her from the family portrait. Why had her sister managed to employ a romantic ruse successfully, while Juliet had fallen short of the mark? Probably because Philip had been willing to cooperate, whereas Cody hadn't. Obviously, the man hadn't found her attractive enough to ruin —at least not publicly at any rate. Perhaps the unflattering gossip she dreaded was all too accurate and she would end up on the shelf after all.

AUGUSTUS DISMISSED his cab after he emerged from the Beaucroft residence, choosing to walk the two miles back to Mayfair so he'd have time to think. As he walked along the pavement, however, he decided to call on Lady Lovejoy before returning home. If he was obliged to wed Miss Gryphon, he oughtn't put off meeting her any longer. Indeed, since he had his grandmother's ring in his pocket, he'd present it to the girl, along with his proposal. Hopefully, he'd muster up some warmth and enthusiasm, despite his lack of sentiment. No doubt Miss Gryphon would be equally apprehensive about him, and he didn't want to seem resentful or ungentlemanly. After all, she wasn't the cause of his problems...only the solution.

Juliet had managed to soothe his distress admirably, in the

uncanny way she'd always had. Although it was difficult for him to view his economic disaster as providential, deep down he suspected she was right about their romance. Their marriage would have been comfortable and harmonious, to be sure, but Juliet deserved better than to marry a man with such an imperturbable nature. Since he so completely lacked passion, an arranged marriage was probably the perfect fit. His wife wouldn't expect him to display any fervent ardor for her, and he wouldn't feel compelled to engage in pretense. After all, not every couple could be fortunate in love.

He veered into Hyde Park on his way to Lady Lovejoy's Mayfair residence. Not more than a half minute later, he saw a pup racing toward him, trailing a rope. Running behind him was presumably the creature's owner, a pretty young woman clad in a billowing baby blue gown with white trim. In the distance, a plump older lady in a plain gown and apron was struggling to catch up.

When the young lady spotted Augustus, her expression grew animated and she waved her arms. "You there! Will you catch my dog?"

He knelt as the little terrier mix approached, intending to catch him, but the pooch made no effort to evade his grasp. Instead, the creature jumped up to lick Augustus's face. Chuckling, the earl picked up the winsome pup and waited for the girl to arrive.

"Oh, thank you!" She took the squirming animal from Augustus. "The little devil got away from me back there and I was worried he'd be crushed by a horse or carriage."

Augustus eyed the slender rope she was using for a leash. "You might want to loop the rope around your hand."

"Yes, that's a good suggestion." She wrapped the end of the rope around her gloved fingers several times. "Now he can't escape!"

As she laughed, he couldn't help but admire her white teeth, lustrous dark hair, and snapping blue eyes. He couldn't place her peculiar accent, but there was no opportunity to ask about it. The girl's maid had arrived, huffing and puffing from her exertions, and was giving him a level look. Of course, he took no offense at the rebuke. Having not been properly introduced to the young lady, he was committing a breach of etiquette by engaging her in conversation.

Augustus lifted his hat and sketched a courtly bow. "Good afternoon."

The brunette curtsied. "Good afternoon." When she smiled at him, a pair of dimples appeared in her creamy complexion.

He continued on his way, a slight smile on his lips. Would his future bride more closely resemble the vivacious, attractive young woman he'd just encountered, or her dour, plump maid? Perhaps it was best to expect the latter and hope for the former.

ALTHOUGH THE PUPPY whined to be let down, Stephanie was fearful of his safety and decided to hold him in her arms until she and her maid, Emma, had crossed the busy street adjacent to Hyde Park and arrived safely on the far side. Having reached the pavement, she allowed the dog to continue the rest of the way at the end of the leash. Although she was enjoying the outing, her poor maid was blotting moisture from her forehead with a bit of cloth.

"How much farther is it, Miss Gryphon, if you don't mind me asking?"

Stephanie produced Juliet's letter so she could refer to the return address on the back.

"I don't exactly know, but the butler told me it was only a short walk from Hyde Park to Belgrave Square."

Emma rolled her eyes. "Mr. Yeats has longer legs than most."

The maid's comment reminded Stephanie of the tall man she'd passed a few minutes before.

"That gentleman in Hyde Park had a very kindly manner, wouldn't you say?"

A sound of assent. "That he did."

"He was rather handsome, too, in an elegant fashion."

"That he was."

Stephanie frowned. "If only my future husband were turn out to be half so amiable, I wouldn't mind being married to him."

"I wouldn't worry overmuch. Didn't you say Miss Beaucroft praised Lord Elbourne to the skies?"

"Yes, but she was likely only trying to make me feel better. What sort of friend would she be to frighten me with the truth?"

The dog yanked on the leash and Stephanie hastened forward. Fortunately, the Beaucrofts' address was only a short distance off and easy to locate. As she knocked on the door, she glanced down at the happy pup wiggling at her feet. Hopefully, Juliet would think the dog was as winsome as she did.

Juliet was sealing a letter to Kitty when a maid came to the drawing room to announce Miss Gryphon's arrival. Almost before she could stand, a gamboling puppy streaked into the room and begged for attention. Stephanie appeared shortly thereafter with an apologetic smile.

"I'm so sorry! I let him slip away from me again, I'm afraid."

"Who is this pretty fellow?" Juliet sat down again and let the creature jump into her lap.

"I haven't named him yet. I rather thought you might like to do it, if you wish to keep him."

Startled, Juliet blinked. "Keep him?"

"Lady Lovejoy's coachman's dog had puppies a month ago,

and he's been trying to find homes for them. I chose one of the girls, whom I named Texas, and brought the boy to you. I thought a new puppy might help take your mind off of Hamlet."

Juliet's heart melted. "That's so thoughtful!" She studied the dog a moment. "I'll call him Robin Hood."

She set the dog down and gave Stephanie a warm smile. "Thank you."

"You're welcome." She glanced over her shoulder at a stout maid lingering in the doorway. "Emma, will you take Robin Hood to the kitchen? Perhaps one of the servants can find a box where the dog can sleep, and you might have a glass of water."

"Yes, Miss Gryphon."

Emma retrieved the pup's leash and led him from the room. Juliet gestured toward a sofa and invited Stephanie to sit.

"Mama should be back from shopping directly. Will you stay for tea?"

As Stephanie shook her head, her curls danced. "I'm afraid I can stay only a few minutes since Lady Lovejoy is expecting me back directly." She smoothed her skirt. "I'd like to take all the credit for Robin Hood, but giving you the puppy was actually my brother's idea."

Juliet's eyebrows rose. "Oh?"

"Cody asked me not to say anything, actually, but I thought you ought to know. My brother might not be the most serious man where romance is concerned, but he can be kind."

"Please thank him for me. It's a shame you weren't here fifteen minutes earlier. Augustus came to call."

"I'm sorry to have missed him." She frowned. "I confess, I'm becoming increasingly apprehensive about meeting Lord Elbourne. I know you admire him greatly, but what if he doesn't like me? Papa will be crushed."

"Why? I understand your father hasn't even met Augustus yet."

"Since Papa is a second son with only a courtesy title, his

heart is set on my marrying into nobility. Rather, he promised Mama to see me wed to aristocracy."

"Augustus will adore you…in due time."

"Do you think so?"

"I've heard arranged marriages can be some of the happiest ones."

Stephanie looked at her askance. "How would you feel if it were you?"

"I suppose it would depend on the person. Since I know Augustus very well, I honestly believe you two will suit one another."

Stephanie frowned. "My father has all but ordered me to fall in love with him."

"And so you shall, Stephanie. I'm sure of it. Come have a look at one of his sketches. Papa had it framed."

Juliet brought Stephanie next to the fireplace, where a myriad of artwork had been hung, and pointed at one of the drawings. "This is Augustus's work."

As Stephanie examined it, she made a sound of admiration. "Why…he's captured you perfectly." Her gaze shifted to the Beaucroft family oil painting over the fireplace mantle. She pointed to the young brunette girl depicted therein. "Is that your sister?"

"Yes, Kitty's a famous beauty, and we're quite proud of her."

"She's very lovely, but her coloring is vastly different from yours. I think I prefer your looks over hers, actually."

"You're all politeness, I'm sure."

"No, I'm not just being polite." Stephanie tweaked one of Juliet's curls. "How fortunate you are to have hair that shade. I believe my brother referred to it as Palomino gold."

"Did he?"

"Cody also said under certain lights it's almost flaxen. I believe he finds it quite arresting."

"I'm sure you're wrong." Juliet hoped she wasn't blushing. "I can't imagine he's given my hair any thought whatsoever."

"I don't mean to pry, but did you two quarrel last night?"

Her eyes widened. "Why not at all. Your brother didn't say anything to the contrary, did he?"

"Oh, no. It's just you both seemed so distracted after dinner."

"Since the Season is rapidly coming to a close, perhaps we're both feeling a little sad." Juliet smiled. "I'm to visit Kitty in Grovebrook in a few days. You're most welcome to come with me if you have no other plans. I'd enjoy your company very much."

"Thank you! I'll ask Papa, but he hasn't mentioned anything. If I can, I'd love to come."

"Good."

TROUBLE

*L*ady Lovejoy's butler gestured toward a pair of open doors. "I'll let the countess know you've come to call, Lord Elbourne."

"Thank you, Yeats."

After Augustus passed through the entrance hall and into the spacious drawing room, he was shocked to discover Lord Gryphon standing behind an easel next to a window.

The earl's eyes narrowed and his knuckles tightened. "You've got a nerve, showing your face here!"

The man glanced up, startled. "I beg your pardon?"

To Augustus's utter embarrassment, he realized he'd been mistaken as to the stranger's identity. "Oh…please forgive me. I thought you were someone else."

"Lord Gryphon, by chance?"

"Why, yes."

"You wouldn't be the first man in London to mistake me for him. I've been challenged to several duels since I arrived here." The man bowed. "I'm Cody Gryphon. Zachary Gryphon is my cousin."

So this was his future brother-in-law? "Lord Elbourne."

Augustus bowed. "Again, I apologize for my rudeness. I'm afraid your cousin and I left things very badly between us not too long ago. I don't wish to give offense, but I must be perfectly frank about it."

"I'm not offended. The last I saw Zachary we were still wearing short pants. He was a rapscallion then, too." He chuckled. "It's been over seventeen years and I'm still being blamed for his transgressions."

Augustus crossed the room. "I'm pleased to make your acquaintance." His gaze fell to the easel. "You draw?"

"Er…this is my first stab at it." Cody gave his handiwork—an awkward still life of a fruit bowl—a dubious glance. "I'm just a beginner."

Augustus examined the sketch. "See here, your subject is a bit ambitious for a beginner. He reached for the fruit bowl on the adjacent table and picked up an apple. "You might start with something like this. And think about drawing the negative space around your subject instead of the apple itself."

A furrow formed on Cody's forehead. "I hadn't thought about it that way. Perhaps you'll make an artist out of me yet."

Augustus bit back a smile. "I wouldn't go that far."

Cody burst into good-natured laughter.

"Is your sister at home?"

"Why no, she's gone on an errand, and my father is out looking at houses. How did you know we were staying with Lady Lovejoy?"

"Miss Beaucroft, mentioned it. I've just come from speaking with her."

"Really? I'm surprised you didn't run into Stephanie. She was going to the Beaucroft residence to deliver a puppy."

Augustus was taken aback. "By any chance, was your sister wearing a blue dress, and was she accompanied by a maid in high dudgeon?"

"Yes, to both questions." Cody peered at him. "Then you must have seen Stephanie?"

"We've not been formally introduced, but we did meet in Hyde Park." Augustus's thoughts slid agreeably to the brief encounter. "I'm sorry I didn't know who she was at the time."

Cody gave him an appraising glance. "So…you intend to marry her?"

"Why yes, if she'll have me."

"She's a bit headstrong about the whole arrangement, and won't give her assent until after she's met you.

"I approve of her caution wholeheartedly. It shows a great deal of intelligence and spirit."

Before Cody could reply, Lady Lovejoy appeared. "Lord Elbourne, how kind of you to call! I see you've met Mr. Cody Gryphon. He and his family have recently arrived in town from overseas."

The countess invited him to sit, and for several minutes she prattled on about the end of the Season. Although Augustus ventured the occasional remark, Cody said little. No doubt the man was trying to take his measure, the better to report back to his sister.

Lady Lovejoy pressed him for details about how his brother, Philip, and Kitty were getting along together. Augustus gave her vague answers, but that didn't seem to bother her at all.

"Such a beautiful couple was never seen, Mr. Gryphon. It's too bad you weren't in London for the wedding." The countess pouted. "Such a shame about Lord Trestlebury's daughter, though. I understand the poor man's not come to terms with Prudence marrying down."

"Philip writes that our cousin Prudence is extraordinarily happy." Augustus shrugged. "Lord Kirkham is a devoted husband and a very amiable fellow. I truly hope Trestlebury accepts him before too long."

Although he would have liked to linger until Stephanie

returned, he had no wish to gossip further about his family. He reached for his hat and stood. "Excuse me, but I must be going."

Cody rose as well. "I'm sorry you've missed my sister."

"As am I. Please convey my sincere desire to make her acquaintance."

The countess stood. "I hope you plan to attend Lord Ferndale's ball tomorrow night? Mr. Gryphon and Miss Gryphon will be there, and Lord Horatio is to escort me."

"I'm looking forward to it." Augustus exchanged a brief glance with Cody. "It should be rather eventful."

CODY PUT DOWN HIS PENCIL, stepped back, and peered at his drawing with dismay. Although it was supposed to look like a shiny, perfect apple, it more closely resembled a piece of rotting fruit. Rather, it appeared to be a child's drawing of a rotten apple, without any sort of artistic merit whatsoever. Scowling, he wadded the paper up into a ball and tossed it into the fireplace. He'd never shown any artistic ability before, so what had made him think he would do any better now? Certainly, nothing about him seemed to appeal to Juliet.

Stephanie appeared in the doorway of the drawing room. "Hello!" She removed her hat, tossed it onto a table, and took a seat on the sofa. "Juliet adored the dog and said you were very thoughtful to think of her."

"You told her it was my idea, did you? In that case, I'm surprised she accepted him."

"Why not?"

Nothing would induce him to mention that scene in the library. "Er...because you've blackened my name to her quite dreadfully. Thanks to you, she has reason to think I'm a rake."

"Well, you are."

"No, I'm not!"

"You're four and twenty years of age and have never been serious about a girl in your life."

"That doesn't mean I'm a rake. I just haven't yet met the right girl."

Stephanie's mouth formed an O. "You're not suggesting Miss Beaucroft is the right one, are you?"

"Don't be absurd." Cody decided to change the subject as quickly as possible. "By the way, Lord Elbourne was just here."

She gasped and her eyes grew wide. "He was? Quick, tell me everything about him!"

"He's a complete troll, I fear." Cody shook his head with mock sorrow. "Curly molars, hairy knuckles, and the smell nearly knocked me senseless at twenty paces."

"Oh, stop!"

He laughed. "I'm teasing, of course. You met him yourself, in Hyde Park. Apparently you had a conversation about the pup."

"No!" Her eyes grew even wider. "That was Lord Elbourne?" She squealed with glee as she jumped up and down.

"I take it you're pleased?"

She ignored his inquiry. "Did he say anything about me? Did he think me pretty?"

"We didn't discuss your appearance, but you evidently made an impression since he asked if you were wearing a blue dress."

"Did you like him?"

Cody could hear the eagerness in her voice. "Very much. Elbourne is everything Miss Beaucroft said he was. Furthermore, he said he was looking forward to meeting you at the Ferndale ball."

His sister's expression grew dreamy. "I'll wear my most splendid gown, and my hair must be magnificent."

"He's already seen you, Stephanie. Besides which, there's little you can do to improve on perfection."

"Thank you, kind sir." She giggled. "I just might be the luckiest girl in England!"

~

SINCE THE FERNDALE ball was the final event of the Season, Mr. Beaucroft had agreed to escort his wife and daughter to the event. Mrs. Beaucroft had taken several days to mourn the loss of Juliet's impending engagement to Augustus and was beginning to suggest other eligible noblemen to her. Even in the carriage on the way to the party, she was counting off possibilities on her kidskin-gloved fingers.

Finally, Juliet had had enough. "Mama, for all intents and purposes, the Season is finished and we must face the fact I haven't managed to secure a husband. That being said, it's only my first Season and there's always next year."

"Yes, but after your sister's rather scandalous courtship, your engagement to an earl would have lifted the family to another level entirely." She pouted. "With so few earls to choose from, I'm afraid we'll have to lower our sights to a viscount. Under no circumstances, however, should you go lower than a baron. That would be insupportable."

"And what if I should choose a terribly wealthy gentleman with no title at all?"

Her father chuckled. "A sizable amount of wealth might take the sting away as far as I'm concerned."

Her mother made a sound of disgust. "Don't you care about your legacy? Why shouldn't your grandchildren be aristocrats?"

Juliet averted her eyes. "That's exactly how Stephanie's father feels."

"Don't lump me in with that social climber!"

Mr. Beaucroft chuckled. "I believe it was Shakespeare who wrote, 'The raven chides blackness.' The phrase fits in this case."

Juliet bit back a smile, but Mrs. Beaucroft seemed to swell with umbrage. "I'm nothing at all like Lord Horatio!"

He patted his wife's hand. "Not at all, dearest. At any rate,

I'm glad the Season is at an end. I long to return to the country and leave the delights of town for another year."

"Kitty invited me for a visit to Constance Hall, Papa. I hope you haven't forgotten?"

"That's right." He nodded. "You have my permission to go, so long as you take that puppy with you."

"Of course! I couldn't bear to be parted from Robin Hood. Also, Stephanie may accompany me, if she has no plans."

"You're a better person than I," her mother murmured. "I can scarcely bear to look at the girl who's ruined your chance of happiness."

Juliet lifted her chin. "Since she provides the means by which the Butler estate can be saved, I can look at her all day long. Besides which, I like her."

Her mother glanced out the window. "There's no accounting for taste, I suppose."

As CODY WAITED with Stephanie in the receiving line, he could tell his sister was nervous by the way she clutched his arm.

"Are you all right?" He gave her a crooked grin. "Do you feel an attack of the vapors coming on?"

"Oh, hush. I'm just excited to meet Lord Elbourne."

"Try to remain calm, if you can. He's a rather nice troll, as trolls go." At Stephanie's sound of frustration, he laughed. "Did I say troll? I meant chap. The digraph at the beginning of both words sound quite similar to my ear."

"Stop teasing me!"

"Sorry. I'll try to behave." He glanced at her pale lilac gown, which was the same shade as her short gloves. "You look absolutely beautiful this evening, may I say? Although your neckline is perhaps a trifle low."

His criticism elicited a giggle. "You think all my necklines are too low, even when they're up to my chin."

When Cody was introduced to Lady Ferndale a few moments later, the older woman peered at him. "Merciful heavens, but I mistook you for Lord Gryphon!"

He hoped his smile covered his irritation. "Yes, milady. Although I haven't spoken with Cousin Zachary in many years, I'm told our current resemblance is uncanny."

He presented his sister to Lady Ferndale, and thereafter they joined Horatio in the entrance hall, where crowds of beautifully-gowned women and dashing gentlemen were chatting in groups or pairs.

Their father rolled his eyes. "Lady Lovejoy has gone off to make the rounds and left me to my own devices."

"Have you seen Lord Elbourne?" Cody asked. "Perhaps he's already in the ballroom."

Stephanie bit her lip. "He might not be here yet."

"I'll locate Lord Moregate. He'll have a better idea when his son will arrive." Horatio excused himself.

As the man strode off, Cody's sister gave him a sympathetic glance. "I expect you've become sick of hearing how much you resemble Zachary."

"It wouldn't be so bad if our cousin had a sterling character. As it is, I seem to remind people of an unpleasant smell." He frowned. "The longer I remain in London, the more attractive Texas seems."

"Once everyone gets to know you, it will be different."

"I won't be in England long enough to care." Over Stephanie's shoulder, he saw a familiar couple approaching. "Prepare yourself, sister. You're about to meet the earl."

"If you're joking, I'll—"

His sister's threat was interrupted by the arrival of Juliet and Augustus. Juliet's stunning ball gown was also cut off the shoulder, similar to Stephanie's, but Cody enjoyed the view far more.

The white satin concoction, with its elaborate pearl trimmings and aquamarine ribbons, served Juliet's delicate coloring to perfection. Cody's mouth went dry.

"Miss Stephanie Gryphon, may I present Augustus Butler, the Earl of Elbourne?" Juliet said. "Augustus, this is Miss Gryphon."

The earl bowed and Stephanie dipped into the low curtsy she'd been practicing. Cody was impressed by how unstudied his sister managed to make it appear.

Juliet continued, "Lord Elbourne, I understand you've already met Mr. Cody Gryphon?"

The gentlemen bowed to one another.

Augustus's eyes crinkled as he gave Cody a smile. "How are your drawings coming along?"

"I must admit, I'm thoroughly convinced my talents lie elsewhere."

"If you enjoy it, that's all that matters." The earl's gaze returned to Stephanie. "I believe we have a bit of time before the dancing begins. Might I challenge you to a game of billiards?"

She was visibly startled. "How did you know I enjoy billiards?"

"A mutual friend." He winked at Juliet.

"Why, I'd adore a game of billiards..." Stephanie gave him a teasing glance "...if you're prepared to lose graciously."

Augustus offered her his arm. "I am if you are."

As the earl and Stephanie strolled off together, Juliet gave Cody a brief curtsy. "If you'll excuse me."

"Miss Beaucroft, please wait." Although she paused, she didn't meet his gaze. "I apologize for what I did the other night. It was ungentlemanly, and I don't reflect on my behavior with satisfaction."

Her face became rosy, and he stifled the impulse to touch the curve of her cheek.

"Thank you, Mr. Gryphon, but I thought we agreed not to

mention it again. Besides which, your point was well taken. I shouldn't have attempted to salvage my reputation with a ruse, especially not at your expense. I stand corrected."

"I feel certain the damage to your reputation from being passed over will prove nonexistent. I imagine when it becomes generally known the earl is courting another lady, you'll hear a collective sigh of relief from half the gentlemen in London."

Juliet finally raised her eyes to his. "That was a kind thing to say."

"I speak the truth." He gave her his best puppy dog look. "Am I forgiven?"

Her mouth turned upward at the corners. "Perhaps a very little, but only because of my regard for Stephanie."

"Aha! I have a great deal of regard for Stephanie, too, so we have that in common. I daresay we should explore our commonality a little further, *señorita*."

Her smile faded. "Stop flirting with me, Mr. Gryphon. Since you're returning to Texas, we both know it can lead nowhere."

Before he could say anything more, she moved off into the crowd with a swish of satin and the rustle of petticoats. Cody frowned as he watched her walk away in iridescent glory. She was perfectly right in what she'd said, of course. He'd made no secret of his plans for the future, so why did he feel as if she'd slapped him across the face yet again? The blame was his for trying to engage her in conversation. After his apology, he should have excused himself and retired to the bar for a drink. Instead, he was rooted to the spot like some sort of lovesick swain, yearning for her to glance back at him.

For a moment, he thought Juliet might have done so, but then his view was cut off by the approach of his father. The older man seemed distracted for some reason.

"I couldn't find Lord Moregate, I'm afraid."

"Don't be concerned. Lord Elbourne was here after all. He and Stephanie are getting acquainted over a game of billiards."

Although his father nodded, the crease between his eyebrows didn't lessen. Cody was puzzled. "Is something amiss?"

"I saw my brother and his wife when I went into the ballroom."

"Uncle William and Aunt Zinna? I didn't even realize they were in town."

"Nor did I. To be frank, after your grandfather disinherited William, I thought I might never see him again. We've never been especially fond of one another."

"I take it your reunion was not a happy one?"

"From the cold manner in which he and Zinna greeted me, I fear they mean to make trouble."

"How?"

"I don't know, but I have a bad feeling about it." He shook his head. "Just stay vigilant."

Augustus tapped in the winning shot, straightened, and gave Stephanie a smile. "Game and match."

She watched as he re-racked the balls. His impeccably tailored evening clothes fit him perfectly, and his air of quiet competence fit him even better.

"You didn't let me win."

"I respect you far too much for that. I hope you're not disappointed?"

"On the contrary, I find it flattering."

"I'm glad. I appreciate a lady who stands on her merits." When he regarded her, it had the effect of a physical caress. "We're in a strange situation, you and I."

"Indeed, we are. I confess, I was rather determined not to like you before."

"And now?"

She lowered her lashes. "I'd say I've been pleasantly surprised."

"As have I." He offered her his arm. "Shall we join the party? The dancing will begin soon and I hope to dazzle you on the dance floor."

She stole a glance at his profile as they strolled from the billiards room. "I'd hoped it would be you."

His eyebrows rose in response. "In what way?"

"When we met in the park the other day, I wished you were Lord Elbourne. I didn't know who you were, of course, but you had a sense of kindness about you I found very appealing."

"I'd no idea who you were either, but you were a bright spot in an otherwise difficult afternoon." He paused. "Did Juliet like the puppy?"

"Oh, yes. Her dog Hamlet ran away, and she was distraught."

"Hamlet?" Augustus seemed puzzled.

"Yes. Cody and I both thought a new puppy would lift her spirits."

"I'm quite confused. Juliet has never had a dog."

"No?" Stephanie was taken aback. "Well, I can only take her at her word. She *was* genuinely upset about something."

"In that case, a puppy was just the remedy."

It was odd that Augustus wouldn't have known about Juliet's dog, Hamlet, but in the excitement of the evening, Stephanie brushed the inconsistency aside. As they moved through the hallway, eyes followed their progress and whispered conversations erupted after they'd passed by. She could only assume a man of Augustus's stature was a fascinating subject amongst society.

As they took their place on the dance floor, she leaned closer. "Do you always create such a stir?"

"It is you who has created a stir, Miss Gryphon. Since it's the last ball of the Season, and I'm the highest ranking bachelor in attendance, the unmarried lady I choose for the first dance takes on special significance. The guests may very well assume I intend to propose to you."

"All that, just from a dance?"

"Let's remove any doubt regarding my intent, shall we?"

He lifted her hand and deposited a lingering kiss on the back of her glove. Even though the marriage was supposedly a foregone conclusion, Stephanie blushed.

Augustus gave her a sidelong glance. "Have I overstepped the mark?"

She felt a delicious tingle travel down her spine. "No. I'd say you hit it perfectly."

WICKED

Cody and his father returned to the ballroom, where the first dance was already underway. He scowled when he realized Juliet was dancing with an eager young man who was holding her altogether too close for propriety. Why hadn't he thought to claim the first dance for himself? In fact, he'd delayed so long he might already be too late to claim any.

When Horatio introduced Cody to his aunt and uncle, whom he scarcely remembered, he could feel the chill his father had referenced. Lord Kesselbury's features had been bloated by an excess of drink over the years, and Lady Kesselbury's plush frame and ruddy complexion were ill served by an overly tight puce gown.

"It's been a long time, lad, but I would have known you anywhere." Lord Kesselbury's voice was flat. "You and Zachary could almost be twins."

"Indeed." Lady Kesselbury gave Cody a tight smile. "I rather think, however, you're far more cheerful than Zachary, at present. You're definitely far more fortunate."

Cody exchanged an uncomfortable glance with his father before venturing a response.

"Er…where is Zachary these days?"

His aunt's lips tightened. "He was forced to return from his Continental tour when his grandfather cut off his allowance without any warning whatsoever. I've begged him to come home, of course, but he's bitter and refuses to have anything more to do with the family. Now the poor boy is languishing in a small apartment on the east side of town, dispirited beyond measure. We're at the end of our rope."

"Perhaps I'll visit him."

"Would you? That's terribly kind." Kesselbury produced a calling card from an inside pocket with an address written on the back. "Zachary needs all the friends he can muster."

His wife flapped her hands at him. "Don't go on about it, dear. Considering Cody and Zachary are blood relatives, it's the least he can do."

"That's so. I'm also reminded that Cody is to inherit an undeserved fortune from his grandfather one day. Everything that would have been Zachary's will be his, instead." Kesselbury sighed. "The knowledge of such injustice must weigh heavy on his conscience."

Cody gritted his teeth as he slid the card into a pocket. "Actually, I've never given it much thought." He hadn't been long in their company, but Lord and Lady Kesselbury struck him as rather despicable. It was no wonder the Gryphon brothers had never been close.

Lady Kesselbury glanced around. "Is Stephanie here? I'd like to meet my niece. She was a babe in arms when I saw her last."

Horatio nodded toward the dance floor. "She's dancing with Lord Elbourne."

Her eyebrows rose. "*That* girl is Stephanie? Why, she turned out prettier than I might have imagined, and quite like her mama." She snickered. "Poor Miss Beaucroft."

Cody's bristled at his aunt's mean-spirited jab. "Why do you say that?"

"Everyone knows Miss Beaucroft had her heart set on marrying Lord Elbourne."

"I beg to differ. Miss Beaucroft feels nothing but sisterly affection for the earl and is great friends with Stephanie. Should Lord Elbourne and Stephanie happen to announce their engagement, Miss Beaucroft will be delighted."

Despite his defense of Juliet, Cody could see neither his aunt nor his uncle believed the truth of his assertions. Would anyone? His fears increased when Lady Lovejoy paused to greet him as she circulated through the party guests.

"Your sister has made quite an impression on Lord Elbourne, I see. Poor Miss Beaucroft's heartbreak is all anyone is talking of." She shook her head and sighed with genuine regret. "How terrible for her, to be thrown over for her friend! I feel rather responsible for introducing them."

"Lady Lovejoy, please believe me when I say Miss Beaucroft's heart is perfectly whole."

She patted his hand. "You're a loyal friend and a gentleman, and I'd expect you to say nothing less."

As she hastened off, Cody began to wonder if Juliet's proposed ruse hadn't been the best course of action after all. She'd certainly guessed correctly that the gossips would be unkind. Furthermore, how would Stephanie react if ugly remarks about Juliet and Augustus got back to her? His eyes flickered toward his aunt and uncle, whose hardened expressions convinced him they would be sure to repeat the rumors to their niece at the first possible opportunity.

Cody watched his sister dancing with Elbourne—an adoring look on her face. In turn, the earl seemed to be wrapped up in her gaze. If he wasn't greatly mistaken, the two of them were well on their way to falling in love, and he meant to see that nothing derailed their courtship and impending engagement.

He must speak with Juliet before it was too late.

~

JULIET CURTSIED at the end of the first dance and applauded the orchestra's efforts. As her partner led her off the floor, she could see Cody making his way in her direction. Did he mean to mock her again with his flirting? Although she kept her countenance, inwardly she braced herself for the impact of his presence. When he reached her side, she was obliged to introduce him to her escort.

"Mr. Waters, have you met Mr. Gryphon?"

Waters gaped at Cody. "Good heavens, but I thought you were Lord Gryphon!"

Cody glared. "Really? I've not heard that before." His retort was edged with sarcasm.

"Well, I-I beg your pardon." Flushed bright red, Waters bowed, edged backward, and disappeared into the crowd.

Juliet gave Cody an even glance. "Must you frighten away all my friends? Mr. Waters is a very sweet man and doesn't deserve your ire."

"Perhaps not, but that's not important right now. Please come with me."

To her surprise, he took her by the hand and tugged her toward the exit. She was compelled to fall into step beside him, to avoid drawing even more attention to his actions.

"You're making a spectacle of me, Mr. Gryphon! Please let go!"

He took her hand and wrapped it around his arm. "Is that better?"

"No. Where are we going?"

"Somewhere private."

Several people stared as they passed, and Juliet gave them a bland smile. Why was Cody embarrassing her this way? He led her out into the garden, until the darkness seemed to swallow them whole. When he finally came to a stop, she snatched her hand away from his arm.

"You've completely shredded my reputation, sir!"

"It doesn't matter."

"What?"

"No, I don't mean that the way it sounds. What I mean to say is, you were right before, about the ruse."

She looked at him, annoyed. "Thank you for admitting you were wrong, but it's too late. Now that Stephanie and Augustus have been seen dancing together, my ruination will be seen as a desperate attempt to make him jealous."

"You misunderstand me. Ruination doesn't go far enough, and I would never have agreed to it in any case. We must become engaged tonight. Immediately, in fact."

Had Cody lost his mind? "Engaged? To what purpose?"

"The gossips say you and Lord Elbourne were going to announce your engagement. If Stephanie hears as much, she'll call the whole thing off. I know for a fact my sister would never marry a man she thought was already spoken for. Stephanie has too much pride."

"Even if we're supposedly engaged, how would that disprove Augustus's feelings for me?"

"It won't, but I believe he's more than capable of persuading Stephanie of his devotion. Besides which, our engagement will take the wind of the gossip's sails. Half their delight is in watching your heartbreak."

She stood with her arms akimbo. "And how do we get out of the engagement down the road?"

"We'll manage." He shrugged. "I'll return to Texas and you'll naturally tire of a long-distance relationship. You'll throw me over at your convenience and no one need be the wiser."

Juliet studied Cody, whose face was earnest, sincere—and far more handsome than should be allowed. Although she gave him credit for trying to help Stephanie, an engagement ruse posed more peril to her heart than he was aware. Even now, his nearness sent waves of longing through her body and dangerous thoughts flooding into her mind. She cared about Stephanie and Augustus, too, but to enter into such a ruse with Cody Gryphon would be incredibly foolish.

She shook her head. "No."

~

STEPHANIE WAS PRACTICALLY giddy with excitement as she danced with Augustus. His regal bearing and calm manner seemed to bathe him in a patina of glamour, and when she was in his arms she felt as if nothing bad could ever touch her. Furthermore, he was the center of attention wherever he went, as was any woman fortunate enough to be in his company. Never before had she appreciated the naked privilege that came with nobility, and she finally understood why her father had desired it for her and her future children. Augustus Butler, Earl of Elbourne, was erudite, sophisticated, handsome, and kind. It was little wonder Juliet had praised him so highly, and Stephanie was poised to do likewise. Although she wasn't yet in love, she certainly felt warmly enough toward Lord Elbourne to desire more time with him. If he felt differently toward her, he was adept at hiding it.

"I look forward to introducing you to Philip, my younger brother."

"I'll have the chance to meet Lord Philip very soon. Juliet is planning to visit her sister in a few days and has asked me to accompany her."

"That's wonderful news. If I can get away, I'll visit you there." His gaze swept over her frame. "I've never seen a woman ride astride before. I must say, the notion intrigues me."

Stephanie blushed. "What a scandalous thing to say, milord."

"Is it?" He lifted one eyebrow. "I find you devastatingly

attractive, Miss Gryphon. Hopefully, that's not too wicked to admit aloud."

"I shan't breathe a word to anyone." She gave him a slow smile. "Did Juliet tell you all my secrets? I must scold her."

"It's my fault, really. I pressed her for as many details as she could recall so I could woo you properly."

"Your gallantry does you credit. I can't imagine many gentlemen who would bother to woo what's already been promised to them."

"Since you can always refuse the match, I take nothing for granted."

Her lips curved in a mysterious smile, but she made no other response. At that moment, she'd no intention of refusing the match. Nevertheless, it wouldn't hurt to keep the earl in suspense awhile longer.

After the second dance ended, Augustus escorted her off the floor. She glanced toward her father, who was chatting with a couple near the door.

"Lord Elbourne, May I introduce you to Papa?"

"Of course, but I've promised the next dance to Juliet. Might I look for you afterward?"

A prickle of jealousy made Stephanie ashamed of herself. Why shouldn't Augustus dance with her friend? She forced a smile to her lips.

"Please enjoy yourself. We have all night."

When the earl kissed the back of her hand again, tingles traveled up her arm.

"Until then, Miss Gryphon."

As Augustus hastened away to find Juliet, Stephanie took herself to task for momentary pangs of jealousy. Her association with the earl was certainly too new for her to feel possessive… and yet it was difficult not to envy the close relationship he had with Juliet. Even so, her friend had never given her any reason for concern. Not only were any ill feelings on her part disloyal, but petty besides. She would be more confident in herself and leave the darker impulses to lesser beings.

As she approached her father, she had a closer look at his companions. The physical resemblance between the two gentlemen was marked. Horatio glanced up and beckoned her closer. "Lord and Lady Kesselbury, allow me to present your niece, Stephanie."

"Uncle William and Aunt Zinna?" A smile sprang to Stephanie's lips. "I'd no idea you would be here this evening! I'm so delighted to meet you at long last."

Her aunt tittered. "Forgive me, but what a dreadful accent! Cody, at least, manages to sound civilized."

Stephanie's good opinion of the woman evaporated instantly and she had to bite back an impertinent remark.

"Now, dearest, we mustn't make the girl feel self-conscious," Lord Kesselbury said. "After all, she's attracted the attention of Lord Elbourne, just as she is."

"Thank you, Uncle William."

The man smiled at her. "If you're not engaged for the next dance, my dear, would you do me the honor?"

"The honor would be mine, sir."

He led her to the dance floor for a waltz. As the music began, she glanced around, hoping to see Augustus and Juliet. The two had taken their places nearer the orchestra, and seemed to be sharing some sort of joke.

Kesselbury followed her gaze. "Poor Miss Beaucroft."

Stephanie was puzzled. "Why do you say that? Juliet is a dear friend of mine."

"I'd renounce that relationship if I were you. Didn't you know she was supposed to marry the earl?"

"What on earth do you mean? She's never been engaged."

"No, no, there was no formal announcement. Nevertheless, everyone expected the couple to become engaged by the end of the Season. Ask anyone at all and they'll tell you as much."

His words grasped her lungs and squeezed them until she could scarcely draw breath. It couldn't be true. Her mind sifted through recent events as she tried—and failed—to refute her uncle's assertions. On Rotten Row, Juliet had been visibly shaken. She'd said she was worried about a lost dog, but what if that was a lie to cover her disappointment? What if she'd just learned Augustus was to marry Stephanie, and her heart was broken? After all, if the earl had never heard of Hamlet, what were the chances the dog existed?

Her uncle seemed oblivious to her mortification. "If I were you, I'd secure Lord Elbourne as soon as you can, and take an extended honeymoon someplace exotic and beautiful. If you can distract him from Miss Beaucroft long enough, I'm certain he'll fall in love with you in no time."

"Forgive me, but I must have some air."

Stephanie fled the ballroom, hastened down the hall, and emerged onto the patio. To her surprise and relief, her brother was leaning against the stone balustrade, staring out over the garden. "Cody!" As he turned to face her, she ran into his arms and burst into tears.

Juliet and Augustus had not been dancing long when he froze, mid-step. She glanced up at him in alarm. "What's wrong, Augustus?"

"Miss Gryphon just ran from the ballroom, in some sort of distress."

Juliet's eyes widened. "We must go after her at once."

"Yes."

Augustus deftly steered them to the outside of the dance floor, where they melted into the crowd. She followed him to the hallway, but Stephanie was nowhere to be seen. Juliet noticed a footman standing at attention just outside the ballroom.

"Did you see a young lady rush past a few moments ago?"

The servant pointed toward the patio. "She went outside."

Juliet fretted as she and Augustus hastened down the hall. "I wonder what happened?"

"I can't imagine. She and I were getting along splendidly before."

"I'm sure it has nothing to do with you, Augustus."

When they emerged onto the patio, they discovered Stephanie sobbing in her brother's protective embrace. Juliet rushed over to touch her friend's shoulder.

"What's wrong?"

To her utter shock, Stephanie turned on her. "Why didn't you tell me you were in love with Lord Elbourne! I feel like a complete fool!"

Juliet exchanged a bewildered glance with Augustus before responding. "But I'm not in love with him. What would make you think so?"

"That's not what I heard! You two were supposed to be engaged and then I came along and spoiled everything. I'd never consider a man who's in love with you!"

Out of Stephanie's view, Cody grimaced and rolled his eyes skyward.

Augustus intervened. "Miss Gryphon, I love Juliet, but I'm not in love with her. I swear it, on my honor as a gentleman."

Stephanie turned her tearstained face toward Juliet. "And you? Don't bother to deny it. I know you told a falsehood about Hamlet to cover up your broken heart."

"I do deny it. I feel the same way about Augustus as he feels about me! We're dear friends, and that's all there is to it."

"I don't believe you."

Juliet became desperate. "I'm not in love with him because my affections are engaged by someone else!"

"Who?"

"I-I can't say his name. Not just yet."

"Why not? Is he another figment of your imagination, like Hamlet?"

When Juliet gave Cody a supplicating look, he cleared his throat. "Miss Beaucroft doesn't wish to tell you the name, but *I* will. We're in love. I've proposed to her, but she hasn't yet given me her answer."

He held out his hand to Juliet, which she took with a rush of gratitude. Nothing could be permitted to come between Stephanie and Augustus…even if it meant she was forced to agree to a ruse which meant certain disaster for her.

"I love your brother quite desperately, Stephanie, but I didn't want to say so. I thought you'd be angry." Juliet met Cody's gaze. "I want to marry him."

He smiled. "Thank heavens."

Cody pulled her into his arms and pressed a kiss to her forehead, which she thought was a nice touch. Nevertheless, shocked silence ensued.

"This is stupid!" Stephanie blurted out finally. "You hardly know one another!"

Cody chuckled. "Didn't you say with certain people you feel as if you'd known them before? That's how it is with Juliet and me. We were drawn together almost instantly."

Augustus pressed a handkerchief into Stephanie's hands. As she dried her eyes, she still seemed skeptical. "You're quite serious?"

Juliet sighed happily as she relaxed against Cody. "Oh, yes."

Stephanie seemed contrite. "I've overreacted, then, and I apologize. I shouldn't have allowed my uncle to upset me."

Cody stiffened. "Uncle William is responsible for hurting your feelings?" A muscle rippled in his cheek. "Father said he might try to cause trouble of some sort. He's upset about being disinherited."

Stephanie frowned. "It's not as if we asked Grandpapa to change his will."

Augustus reached for Stephanie's hand. "Perhaps now would be a good time for you to introduce me to your father. We'll show Lord Kesselbury he can't come between us."

She gave him a beaming smile and tugged him toward the house. Before Augustus disappeared from the patio he gave Cody and Juliet a surreptitious nod and silently mouthed a thank you.

As soon as they were alone, Juliet stepped away from Cody and took a deep breath to calm her nerves. "I can't believe that worked."

"Lord Elbourne seems aware of what we are up to."

"Yes. He knows me too well to believe I would rush into an engagement with you."

"That sounded suspiciously like an insult."

"No, I just meant I would never rush into an engagement with a relative stranger." Juliet paused. "Thank you for your help just now. It was rather gracious of you, considering my adamant refusal earlier."

"My sister's happiness is my main concern, but I'm glad if I can help you as well. It seems to me that far too many people in society are eager to relish the misery of others."

"Perhaps it's because they are miserable people."

"I imagine you're right." He gave her a crooked grin. "So, we're engaged. Would you like to seal it with a kiss?"

He leaned in so close she caught a whiff of his cologne. Her knees went slightly weak at his masculine scent, but she forced herself to push him away. "Don't joke! This is actually going to be a trifle messy. You'll have to speak with my father and can't predict how he'll respond. My mother, on the other hand, will probably have a fit."

"Because I'm a Gryphon?"

"I shan't lie to you; she detests your cousin, and by extension, your family. In addition, she desperately wants me to marry an aristocrat."

"Perhaps someday you will. In the meantime, however, you're stuck with me."

"I wouldn't put it that way. My mother and I don't share the same standards."

"So theoretically speaking, you'd consider me eligible?"

"Not entirely. Any husband of mine should plan to keep his boots on English soil."

"That rules me out."

"Exactly."

"Well…are you ready to act the happy couple?" Cody held out his arm. "Lead me to your father, then, so I may do the deed properly."

As Juliet laid her hand on his sleeve, she giggled. "This feels terribly wicked."

"And yet, you laugh." He grinned. "I suppose that makes me a bad influence."

IN THE HALLWAY outside the smoking room, Mr. Beaucroft peered at Cody. "What did you say?"

"I realize it's rather sudden, but I wish to marry your d-daughter."

Inwardly, Juliet winced. In the face of her father's towering presence, Cody's customary bravado was noticeably muted. Considering the proposal was a ruse, why was he nervous? After her father turned his attention to her, however, she felt intimidated as well.

"This was what you were hinting at in the carriage, eh?"

Cody raised a surprised eyebrow, but Juliet tried to ignore it.

"I…well, I hadn't anticipated Mr. Gryphon's offer tonight, exactly, but I suppose you could say I was testing the waters."

"Your mother won't be pleased."

Juliet began to fear her father meant to withhold his permission. "Yes, sir. She's made her wishes quite plain."

A broad smile creased her father's face and he burst out into laughter. "We'll just have to bear up under the disapproval, won't we?" He produced a cigar from an inner pocket and thrust it into Cody's hands. "Let's have a smoke. If you're to be my son-in-law, we should get to know one another."

Mr. Beaucroft smacked Cody good-naturedly on the back and steered him toward the smoking room. Cody managed a brief, bewildered glance at Juliet over his shoulder before he disappeared from view. Left alone once more, she decided to go in search of her mother. Although she dreaded the woman's reaction, it was best to get it over with.

*M*rs. Beaucroft was at the buffet in the banquet room, loading a plate with bits of savory meat, roasted vegetables, and Yorkshire pudding.

"Mama, I must speak with you."

Her mother radiated gloominess. "Oh, there you are." She put her plate down and glanced around to make sure no one could overhear. "My worst fears have come to pass. Everyone has noticed Augustus's marked attentions to that Gryphon girl and you've become a laughingstock. After I eat, I think I'll plead a headache so we have a legitimate excuse to leave the ball. Heaven knows, it's not far from the truth."

"There's no need, Mama. Mr. Cody Gryphon has proposed and I've accepted him."

"What?" Mrs. Beaucroft stared. "Your father will never agree!"

"On the contrary, Papa gave him a cigar to welcome him to the family just now. I know this comes as a disappointment to you, Mama, but—"

Her mother shrieked and kissed her on both cheeks. "What a

clever girl! How you managed to save the family from disgrace, I'll never know, but I'm grateful nevertheless." She lowered her voice. "The lad has no title but he's as rich as Croesus!" She paused. "I'll just have to get used to his unfortunate appearance."

As Mrs. Beaucroft hastened off to tell her friends the news, Juliet was taken aback. Not once had her mother asked her about her feelings or questioned why she'd rushed into an engagement. The lack of curiosity was particularly strange considering Kitty had also used an engagement ruse not so long ago. For that matter, her father had seemed to accept the arrangement with uncharacteristic equanimity. Was her mother was more interested in social status and her father more concerned about money than either of them cared about her happiness? Inwardly, Juliet sighed. Although her parents couldn't possibly know it now, none of the Beaucrofts would get want they wanted with this supposed engagement. In the end, she wouldn't become Cody Gryphon's wife, and that was the saddest thing of all.

Lady Lovejoy was gliding toward her with such an overjoyed expression, Juliet knew she must have heard about the engagement.

"Why you slyboots! Here I was, thinking you were going to marry Lord Elbourne when it was Mr. Gryphon who caught your eye. The Beaucroft girls certainly have a propensity for sudden engagements."

"Er...sometimes when you meet the right man, you just know it."

"How terribly romantic. Have you any idea when you might marry?"

"None, I'm afraid. Since the Season is over, however, I'm sure Mr. Gryphon—Cody—and I will have many opportunities to discuss it."

"I'm sure you'll want to confer with your sister." She

frowned. "I still feel embarrassed about taking Kitty's engagement for a ruse, but at least I can make up for it by giving *you* a party."

"That's terribly kind, but wholly unnecessary. I can assure you, no hard feelings exist whatsoever, and Kitty holds you in the highest regard."

"Let me know when you've set a date, and I'll host an engagement party."

"Thank you, Lady Lovejoy. I—"

Juliet and the countess were suddenly surrounded by fellow debutantes. As the girls began to lob questions at her about Mr. Gryphon, Lady Lovejoy gave her a little wink and glided away.

"I can't believe you're the first of us to be engaged!"

"And in your first Season, too!"

"I never thought I'd see a man as handsome as Lord Gryphon—until his cousin arrived."

"When did Mr. Gryphon ask you to marry him, and how?"

As Juliet answered her friends' questions, she was filled with appreciation for Cody's rescue. How vastly different the evening would have unfolded had he not done so.

THE FERNDALE BALL lasted until three o'clock, although only the youngest and hardiest souls stayed the entire time. Mr. Beaucroft dozed off in a library wing chair, and it took several minutes to locate him when it was time to leave. With only a few hours of sleep, Juliet ate her breakfast bleary-eyed and barely awake the next morning. Her father was scarcely any better, but Mrs. Beaucroft was effervescent and buoyant from what she considered to be her triumph the evening before.

Mr. Beaucroft finally gave his wife a quelling look. "You'd think it was *your* engagement with the way you're carrying on."

A raft of letters arrived just then, which the butler carried into the dining room on a large silver tray. Mrs. Beaucroft gave the entire lot a cursory examination.

"The usual *pour prendre congé* notes, of course. Juliet, you'll have to help me write ours after breakfast. We're planning to put you and Miss Gryphon on the train to Grovebrook tomorrow. Your father and I will depart for the country the day after."

"Yes, Mama."

"There are quite a few letters to you this morning. I imagine they're from well-wishers on the news of your engagement. Your father will put a formal announcement in the paper before we leave town."

Juliet glanced through her letters, pausing when she recognized the handwriting on one in particular. For a moment, she thought her eyes must be playing tricks on her.

"What has you so mesmerized?" her father asked.

"Oh, er, it's just a letter from an old friend of mine. She left early in the Season to marry a vicar in her home town."

"A vicar?" Mrs. Beaucroft wrinkled her nose. "She mustn't have been promising, then. What was her name?"

"Um...Ophelia Macintosh."

"I don't remember her at all."

"She wasn't terribly memorable." Juliet pushed back her chair. "May I be excused, Mama? I'd like to read my letters before we get started on our own correspondence."

"Don't take too long."

"I won't. I must dash off a letter to Kitty, telling her to expect me and Stephanie tomorrow afternoon. Augustus is planning to visit Grovebrook as well in a few days."

Juliet gathered the envelopes and rushed upstairs to her bedchamber. When the door was closed, she quickly opened the letter which had seemed to burn her hand the moment she recognized the penmanship.

Dear Juliet,

You're my only hope. I've been cast off by my family and have taken refuge with my great-aunt, Mrs. Agatha Darien, in Little Brambleton. Although she's exceedingly elderly, half blind, and barely gets by, at least she hasn't let me starve.

After all the difficulty I've caused your family, I've no right to ask for your help. But since you've always been a kind and decent girl, perhaps you'll take pity on me. Will you intercede on my behalf with Lord Gryphon? Once Zachary understands he's to be a father before the year is out, I know he'll change his mind and marry me.

If you won't assist me, I've nowhere else to turn.

Very Sincerely,

Violet

So her former friend had finally asked for her help, had she? Juliet frowned and tucked the letter into a book, where it wouldn't be found. Violet Haver had made her own bed. Let her lie in it.

LORD HORATIO PEERED at Cody from behind the closed doors of the library. "I don't want you to imagine I disapprove of Miss Beaucroft in any way. Quite the opposite, in fact."

A smile played around the corners of Cody's lips. "I hear a *but* coming along."

"It's just not like you to behave in such a precipitous fashion, especially where women are concerned. Why did you rush into an engagement on such short acquaintance?"

"For Stephanie's sake, of course. You see, Juliet and I both want to see her marriage to Lord Elbourne go forward without a snag. Thanks to Uncle William, rumors of a romance between Juliet and the earl reached Stephanie last night."

"No!"

"Oh, yes. Juliet and I had to do something drastic to keep things on track."

"Your engagement is a ruse?" Horatio sat back. "I'm quite astonished. Miss Beaucroft is a jolly good sport to go along with it."

"You make it sound as if an engagement to me is a hardship."

"I don't mean it that way and you know it." He frowned. "Your sister would be furious if she knew."

"She won't ever find out. By the time Juliet and I call off our engagement, Stephanie will be happily married and settled into her new life." Cody smiled. "Besides which, didn't you ask me to do whatever it took to bring the marriage about?"

"Yes, and I thank you from the bottom of my heart. My brother's character is fatally flawed, I fear, and he passed his ethics to his son."

"Speaking of Zachary, I'm going to pay him a visit this morning."

"Is that wise?"

Cody shrugged. "Perhaps not, but I'm curious to see how he turned out."

"I caution you not to become overly involved in his problems."

"I won't."

"As for me, I'm still looking at properties and I'd like your opinion when you're free."

"I'm available as soon as I see Stephanie off on the train tomorrow, but why are you in such a hurry?"

"I wish to move from Lady Lovejoy's home as expeditiously as possible." His father gave him a pained glance. "I've no wish to marry again. Neither do I intend to be inveigled into doing so."

"I'm glad to hear it." Cody chuckled. "Neither do I."

"Is that so?" Horatio cocked his head. "I confess, you and Miss Beaucroft played the part of young lovers rather convincingly."

"She considers me a cad and a rake. I'm sure her opinion of me will vastly improve, however, once I'm in Texas."

~

CODY STROLLED THROUGH LEADENHALL MARKET, trying not to look as bewildered as he felt. He disliked not knowing where he was going, particularly when he was surrounded by people who were rushing past like steamships through the ocean. Finally he managed to catch the eye of a stout woman who was examining a rack of plucked chickens available for purchase.

"Forgive me for bothering you, but could you point me toward J. Morris, Butcher?"

"If it's good beef ye want, I'd go ter Yates and Croft."

"Thank you, but I really must find J. Morris."

She jerked her head to the side. "Down this street aways, and turn left at the next intersection. It'll be on yer right."

He tipped his hat. "Much obliged."

A few minutes later he was at J. Morris, Butcher, where sides of butchered beef hung in the windows. As soon as he entered the place, he was obliged to press a handkerchief to his nose in a fruitless attempt to extinguish the noisome smell. Worse, he was forced to watch his step, lest he inadvertently trod upon the dark brown pools of blood that dotted the bare floor.

A clerk approached. "Can I help ye, Guv'nor? Everything ye see is fresh, as of this morning. No better beef to be had in London, even if I say so meself."

Although Cody knew better, he didn't say so. Having spent the last seventeen years in Texas, he was very familiar with cattle—freshly slaughtered or not.

"I was told Zachary works here."

The clerk's eyebrows rose. "Yer acquainted with our Zack?" He gestured toward an open door in the back. "He's in through there. Mind the cutlery."

Cody removed his hat before ducking through the doorway. In the room beyond, burly men were positioned at heavy wooden tables, swinging cleavers and hatchets as they carved steaks and roasts. He spotted Zachary behind the last table, his thick white apron and hands smeared with blood. His cousin sported three weeks' worth of beard, he was exceedingly slender, and his bare head appeared to have been shaved. As Cody approached, Zachary planted his cleaver into the table and gave him a baleful glance.

"I would have known you anywhere, cousin. Forgive me if I don't shake your hand."

Cody hadn't expected Zachary would be glad to see him, so he wasn't surprised by the cold greeting. Nevertheless, it was difficult to know what to say.

"It's been a long time."

"How did you find me?"

"Your landlord. I gave him a crown in exchange for information."

"He gave me up for five shillings? He and I will have to have a word about that."

"Don't hold it against him. I told him we were related and he could see the resemblance for himself." Cody glanced around. "What are you doing here?"

"Working."

"Surely your father gives you an allowance?"

"Not that it's any of your business, but I owe money to people who wish to do me bodily harm. I've changed my appearance, but if I don't pay them back soon, they'll catch up to me sooner or later."

Cody reached for his wallet. "How much do you owe?"

"Put that away, you idiot!" Zachary's voice sounded like a low hiss of steam. "The men who work here are ex-convicts. They'd kill you as soon as look at you."

Cody's hand dropped to his side. "Let me do something. I want to help."

His cousin frowned. "Meet me at the O'Shanty Tavern tonight at seven o'clock and you can buy me dinner."

"Where—"

"Any cab driver will know where it is. Don't show up dressed like that or you'll be robbed."

After a curt nod, Cody left. Outside Leadenhall Market, he hailed a cab to ferry him back to Lady Lovejoy's residence. As the carriage rolled through the streets of London, he wished the stench of blood would leave his nostrils. Even worse was the image of his cousin, wielding a cleaver like a common laborer. He'd been told Zachary had comported himself improperly and was generally reviled by good society, but he'd never been told anything specific. Perhaps when he called on Juliet that afternoon, she'd tell him the real story.

STEPHANIE WAS PLAYING with her puppy in Lady Lovejoy's garden when Cody came out on the patio. She came running, with the dog close on her heels.

He chuckled. "You're finally awake."

"Oh, don't be mean. I was so excited last night, I couldn't fall asleep until dawn. Where have you been?"

"I went to see Zachary."

"How is he?"

"He was just stepping out when I arrived." For some reason, Cody was reluctant to disclose what he'd discovered at the butcher's. "I'm to dine with him tonight."

"Does he resemble you as much as people say?"

"Actually, he's grown a beard, so I couldn't tell." He paused. "I'm going to see Juliet after lunch if you want me to relay a message."

Stephanie gave an excited bounce. "May I go with you?"

He shook his head; the subject of his conversation with Juliet would be best discussed without an audience. "Not this time, I'm afraid."

"That's not fair."

"You'll have a great deal of time alone with Juliet on the train tomorrow, whereas I will only have a few minutes with her this afternoon."

"I suppose you're right, if you put it that way."

"Besides which, Lord Elbourne will likely call on you this afternoon. You'll want to be here to receive him, won't you?"

"Of course. Well, please tell Juliet again how sorry I am for behaving so badly at the ball. I'm heartily ashamed for doubting her."

"I'll tell her, but I don't think she's one to hold a grudge."

Stephanie wrinkled her nose. "You make her sound annoyingly perfect."

"Funny, that's exactly what I said about the earl."

"He *is* perfect, but not annoyingly so."

Cody laughed. "That's exactly what I think about Juliet. Absolutely perfect in every way."

SERVANTS WERE busy preparing the Beaucroft home for a lengthy winter vacancy when Cody came to call. When he suggested Juliet accompany him for a stroll in the garden, she called Robin Hood and let him come along. Although she presumed Cody had something personal to discuss, she was surprised when he asked for details about Lord Gryphon's reputation. While her puppy explored flower beds and chased insects, she related the series of events regarding Zachary's behavior toward Kitty, the trouble it had caused, and the ruse necessitated by his wicked deeds.

Afterward, Cody stared at her, obviously aghast. "Are you sure your information is correct, particularly regarding my cousin's assault on your sister?"

"I saw the bruises myself, and wouldn't rest until Kitty told me everything. And then, after Lord Gryphon told an atrocious lie blaming Philip for the attack, it took the combined efforts of Augustus and my father to publicly refute the claim and turn the tables on him. I assure you, your cousin deserves his notoriety."

Cody sat there, seemingly unmoved, and annoyance crept down her spine.

"You needn't take my word for it. Ask Augustus, and he'll verify everything. Surely you trust *his* veracity and lack of bias." Despite her efforts to the contrary, she failed to keep a tinge of heat from her tone. Did Cody truly think she would invent such a horrid falsehood out of whole cloth, especially when it involved her own sister?

"It's not that I don't believe you, Juliet. It's just that I'm exceedingly shocked. I wish to tell you something in the strictest confidence, which you're not to repeat to anyone. No one, not even my sister and father, knows what I'm about to tell you. Zachary is hiding from creditors and is laboring as a butcher amongst the lowest persons imaginable. When I found him, he was smeared with blood and clutching a meat cleaver."

"You're joking. Lord Gryphon is a popinjay and fastidious to a fault!"

"Surely you don't mean to cast aspersions on my veracity?"

"I-I wouldn't go that far. Like you, however, I'm shocked."

Cody sighed. "I'm meeting with Zachary tonight to see what sort of help I ought to provide. As abhorrent as his actions have been, I can't stand back and let a member of my family suffer."

"I disagree. If he doesn't suffer, he can never feel the consequences of the bad choices he's made. Lord Gryphon deserves to be punished for what he's done."

He peered at her. "That's a rather harsh stance to take, wouldn't you say? If penitence is genuine, shouldn't people be given a second chance?"

"You've no idea what you're talking about. As it so happens, I've just had a letter from the girl he despoiled, begging for my help." Juliet produced Violet's letter, which she'd retrieved from its hiding place and carried with her all day. "I show this to you also in the strictest confidence, and ask you not to share it with anyone."

Cody frowned as he read through the missive. "Zachary's to be a father? This changes everything."

"In what way? I've read that letter a dozen times, trying to decide how I should respond, but I keep coming to the same conclusion. Violet and Lord Gryphon tried to ruin my sister's life and our family name, and I'm determined to leave them to themselves."

"There's a baby involved! Clearly, you have no spark of compassion whatsoever."

Juliet gritted her teeth against the accusation. "Obviously I do, otherwise I wouldn't be struggling with my decision! But since you didn't witness the tears and suffering brought about by Violet's actions, you've no right to judge!"

"But now she's the one suffering. Don't you suppose it cost her a great deal of mortification to beg you for help? I didn't realize anyone could be so hard-hearted."

Any modicum of truth Cody's words held were obscured by his self-righteous idealism. Furthermore, his mischaracterization of her opinions had pushed her too far. Since she was no longer in the mood to be particularly civil, she made no response at all other than fixing her gaze on the pup.

Cody sighed. "Do I at least have your permission to show the letter to Zachary? I think he needs to know what he's done and be encouraged to do the proper thing."

"You're wasting your time, but you have my permission to try."

His bow was curt and perfunctory. "Good day to you, Juliet."

As he left, she drilled holes in his back with her eyes. How dare he try to make her feel guilty? Nevertheless, she viewed his visit as fortuitous. Since he'd managed to make her dislike him more than ever, she'd remind herself of this moment when he departed England. Her aversion to Cody Gryphon would stand her in good stead then.

CONSCIENCE

Since Cody had worked his father's extensive ranch back in Texas, he owned several sets of unremarkable laborer clothes suitable for a visit to a hardscrabble tavern located in a rough neighborhood. Although he'd informed Lady Lovejoy he was dining out, he slipped from her residence without fanfare while everyone else was dressing for dinner. He was obliged to walk several blocks before he found a growler willing to pick him up, but at last he was on his way to O'Shanty Tavern.

As the carriage rolled through the streets of London, he reflected on his visit to Juliet that afternoon. Admittedly, her looks and manner had captivated him before, but his image of her perfection had been shattered by her heartless attitude. He wouldn't have believed her capable of such indifference if he hadn't seen it for himself. Fortunately he'd discovered Juliet's true nature sooner rather than later. Armed with that knowledge, he could shield himself from her charms and stay true to his goal of returning to Texas as a bachelor.

On the other hand, was it entirely fair to expect her to overlook her grievances, especially when they were so fresh? After all, the mischief perpetrated at the hands of Violet and Zachary had not impacted him in the same way as it had her. Granted, he'd been treated with some hostility by those members of society who couldn't disassociate him from his cousin. Nevertheless, that was hardly a disaster. What mitigating circumstances—if any—would his cousin have to offer?

~

ZACHARY SHOVELED beef stew into his mouth like a starved man, and washed it down with dark ale. Although Cody found the food and drink barely palatable, he ate what had been set in front of him to be polite. When his cousin had had his fill, he pushed his empty bowl to one side. Cody could barely make out Zachary's features in the darkened tavern, but his body language radiated angry bitterness.

"So, cousin, have you satisfied yourself I've fallen as low as I deserve?"

"I've not satisfied myself of anything yet. I've heard reports of your behavior toward the Beaucrofts and other women that give me pause."

"Whatever you've heard about me is likely true."

"That's all the response I'm to have?"

Zachary shrugged. "I'm wicked to the core, as is my father, and that's why Grandfather disinherited us. You should be glad of our malfeasance, since it accrues to your family's benefit. Your father will be a very wealthy man someday."

"Misery never makes me glad. Furthermore, my father comes by his own exceedingly vast fortune honestly, by hard work and the sweat of his brow. As a second son, he expected nothing and yet made something of himself by striking out on his own."

His remark earned his cousin's scorn. "What would you know about hard work?" Zachary displayed his roughened calluses and barely healed blisters. "I butcher meat from sunup to sundown, just to earn enough money to pay my gambling debts. I fear for my life, so I don't want to hear about your successes."

Cody displayed his own calluses. "I worked as a *vaquero* on my father's cattle ranch since I was ten years old. I know plenty about hard work, and far more than is suitable for a gentleman. Spare me your bile."

"Touché, cousin." Zachary's smile was grim. "I bow to your noblesse oblige."

Cody's eyes narrowed. "I've never been tempted to thrash anyone as much as I'd like to thrash you right now."

His cousin laughed. "You wouldn't be the first, but I daresay it would do no good."

Cody produced Violet's letter and tossed it onto the table. "Read this."

Zachary slid the candle nearer and unfolded the missive. As he read it, a myriad of expressions crossed his face. Finally, he glanced up. "How did you get this?"

"Miss Juliet Beaucroft gave me permission to show it to you."

He frowned. "I thought Violet was lying to me before when she said she was with child."

"Apparently she wasn't. You must do the right thing and marry the girl."

Zachary shook his head. "She's better off without me, I assure you."

"How can you say that? The lady needs a husband and provider, and your child needs a father!"

"Didn't you hear me before? I'm a wanted man, Cody. Even if I wished to marry Violet, I made enemies out of some dangerous people. I can't put her in danger."

"I'll pay your debts and give you a small stake besides. Isn't a chance at redemption better than hiding the rest of your life?"

Cody slid a dirty rag across the table, wrapped around a stack of pound notes. "This should help."

Zachary stuffed the small bundle into his pocket without bothering to look inside. "I'll take your money because I'm desperate, but I assure you it won't satisfy my creditors. Nevertheless, it'll buy me time."

"How much in the way of funds do you need?"

"No amount of money will smooth over the ill will I've engendered." He glanced at Violet's letter. "May I keep this? It'll be a reminder that somebody loved me once."

After Cody nodded, Zachary slid the envelope into his pocket, reached across the table, and shook his hand. "Thank you, cousin. I probably won't see you again."

Zachary lurched to his feet and strode toward the door. Cody made no attempt to stop him. Maybe the help he'd offered wasn't what his cousin needed. Perhaps Juliet was right and Zachary was just too far gone to save. His attempt to help had ended in failure, he'd wasted his time, and felt foolish to boot. He tossed some coins on the table, drained his ale, and left the tavern.

Cody's accusations about her attitude bothered Juliet more than she'd imagined. That night, she tossed and turned, unable to sleep. He'd made it sound as if she were despicably cruel and unfeeling, although nothing could be further from the truth. Considering everything Violet had done, was Juliet wrong to turn her back to the girl? Besides which, if she came to Violet's aid, wouldn't Kitty view her actions as disloyal in the extreme? She had a duty to her own family, and owed Violet nothing.

And yet, her conscience bothered her still.

If Cody managed to convince Zachary to marry Violet and take proper care of her, that would be all well and good. But what if—as she suspected—he didn't succeed? Violet was living with her elderly aunt, who was barely getting by. Suppose after the baby arrived, the aunt died. Who would take care of Violet and her child then?

Juliet turned on her side so she could stroke Robin Hood, who now refused to sleep anywhere except on her bed. The puppy was fast asleep and dreaming of chasing butterflies, if the tiny movements of his paws were any indication. As she stroked his fur, the pup yawned, stretched, and went back to sleep. Juliet smiled and scratched the back of his ears. The little dog would certainly enjoy running through the fields at Constance Hall during her stay.

Grovebrook was not especially far from Little Brambleton. In fact, Little Brambleton was only one train stop to the north. What if she were to visit Violet, just to see how she fared? A short visit wouldn't necessarily mean she approved of the girl's behavior, but perhaps it was the decent thing to do. Juliet had a sum of money to spare, put by from her allowance. Certainly it would cause very little hardship to her if she gave it to Violet for her expenses. In addition, they could discuss how Violet might make a living for herself going forward.

The only trick would be to get away from Constance Hall without answering awkward questions about her destination. To spare Kitty's feelings, she'd have to keep it secret, of course. Furthermore, she wouldn't want Cody to know, either. Should he learn the truth, his smugness would be unbearable. Besides which, it would be best if he continued to think ill of her. He'd keep his distance that way, and perhaps she wouldn't constantly yearn to feel the softness of his lips against hers. She'd just have to fashion some sort of plausible excuse and hope not to be found out.

As the train pulled out of the station, Stephanie and Juliet tried to get their pups to settle down. Both Texas and Robin Hood wished to look out the window, but the speed at which the scenery sped by made them anxious. Stephanie chucked Texas under her chin, and the little dog wagged her tail.

"I daresay Texas and Robin Hood will relax once they get used to the train," Juliet said.

"I imagine so. Does Robin Hood sleep with you?"

"Of course. After the first night, he wouldn't stop whining until I lifted him onto the coverlet."

"That was the same with Texas. I'm so thankful you invited me to visit with your sister and brother-in-law. It would have been dreadfully dull in town without you."

"I hope it'll be fun. At least you'll be able to see a little more of England."

"Lord Elbourne will join us in a day or two. I do believe I'm quite infatuated with the man."

"And he with you."

"You've been awfully gracious, but I'm still embarrassed about the other night."

"You needn't be. I'm just glad we're beyond it."

Stephanie gave Juliet a worried look. "Did you and Cody quarrel, by chance? You both seemed rather cool to one another at the station just now."

Juliet saw no reason to hide the truth. In fact, it was the perfect opportunity to begin unwinding the ruse. "We did have a disagreement." To her horror, tears began to sting her eyelids.

"Oh, no, I didn't mean to make you cry!"

"It's all right. I didn't realize how upset I was about it until now." Juliet cleared her throat. "We disagreed philosophically about what to do when a former friend asks for help. I took the position that if the person had wronged me, I'd no obligation to render assistance. Cody thought my stance unfeeling. His regard for me has cooled irreparably as a result."

"I'm sure that's not the case, but he's rather stupid to let such a silly argument come between him and the woman he loves. For what it's worth, I happen to agree with you. I'll write and scold him for being officious."

"I beg you not to mention it to him, please. If he doesn't wish to heal the breach, it's best to find it out now. I shouldn't like to spend the rest of my life with a domineering man who won't let me have my own opinion when it differs from his."

"Nor would I. All right, I won't say anything, but I hope he comes around."

Juliet knew differently, but she smiled through her tears anyway. "I'm sure it will work out for the best."

"I'm glad you forgave me for my outburst toward you. I've been trying to decide why I let my jealousy take over. I think it was because I wasn't raised in England and have no idea how to fit in to society here. After I met Lord Elbourne and realized how much I liked him, I rather wondered how there could be anything about me to attract him apart from my money."

"Don't be so hard on yourself for your feelings. I daresay I could never fit in to Texas society."

Stephanie frowned. "My mother always felt the same way. She did the best she could to be a rancher's wife, but it wasn't easy for her."

"I'm sorry for your loss. It must be terribly difficult for you."

"Yes, it's been lonely since her passing. In some ways, it was harder on Cody. Mama was especially close with him, and he became quite undone at her funeral."

"Is that why he's so keen to return to Texas, do you suppose?"

"I hadn't thought about it until now, but I suspect that's it. He's had a very hard time letting her go."

Stephanie's revelation seemed to squeeze Juliet's heart. She couldn't possibly compete with the memory of Cody's revered mother, and she didn't wish to try. Saddened, she pulled Robin Hood into her lap and stroked his fur until he fell asleep.

~

OVER A BREAKFAST of crisp bacon and porridge, Kitty read Juliet's letter with growing concern.

Philip glanced up from his eggs and toast. "You've gone rather quiet. Your sister hasn't postponed her visit, has she?"

"No, she's to arrive this afternoon with her friend. Nevertheless, I can scarcely believe the information in this letter. Had you any notion your father was in financial difficulty?"

An expression of utter incredulity crossed his face. "What? That's absurd!"

"Juliet writes that because of the financial difficulty threatening the estate, a marriage has been arranged between Augustus and a Texian heiress named Miss Stephanie Gryphon."

"Why didn't my father or Augustus tell me any of this?"

"Perhaps they didn't want to worry you." Kitty frowned. "You don't suppose Miss Gryphon is related to the Gryphon family, do you?"

"She must be. I understand Lord Harkencester had a younger son who left England to make his fortune across the Atlantic. I'd no idea the fellow landed in Texas of all places, but Miss Gryphon must be Lord Harkencester's granddaughter and, therefore, Lord Gryphon's cousin."

"Since one cannot choose one's relatives, I shan't hold Lord Gryphon against Miss Gryphon. I confess, however, I'm rather disappointed that Juliet and Augustus aren't to marry. I know she's terribly fond of him."

"I must leave for London immediately after breakfast."

"But we've guests on the way!"

"I'll return as soon as I'm able, but it won't be until after I can get this straightened out. Kitty, I examined the estate's books myself and I'm quite familiar with all its assets. Unless something has gone horribly wrong in the last two months, the estate is solvent."

~

WHEN JULIET and Stephanie arrived at the Grovebrook rail station, Kitty and Prudence were there to greet them. Kitty was as gorgeous as ever, but Juliet wasn't prepared for how plump and beautiful Prudence—now known as Lady Kirkham—had become. Indeed, married life seemed to suit both ladies, and Juliet couldn't have been more pleased. They bid her and Stephanie a warm welcome, and ushered them to the carriage. After the luggage had been loaded, their short journey to Constance Hall began.

"I must apologize for Philip's absence. He's gone to London on business, I'm afraid," Kitty said. "I urged him to return as soon as possible, but it won't be until tomorrow at the earliest."

Juliet was disappointed. "That's too bad, but Stephanie will meet him upon his return."

Prudence gave Texas a pat on the head as she took Robin Hood onto her lap. "Matching pups?"

Stephanie's eyes sparkled with merriment. "There's one significant difference, Lady Kirkham. Texas is a girl and Robin Hood is a boy. Nevertheless, they're litter mates."

"By the way, Stephanie, Prudence's mother and Augustus are first cousins," Juliet said.

"Oh, my! Everybody seems to be related to everyone else in England. I never had any extended family in Texas, so it's all rather complicated to me."

"Miss Gryphon, have you had the chance to meet any of your extended family since your arrival?" Kitty asked.

"Only Uncle William and Aunt Zinna. I'm sad to say, neither one treated me with any particular regard. My brother Cody visited our cousin Zachary the other day, but found little welcome there, either."

Prudence nodded. "Blood isn't always thicker than water. I myself am estranged from my father." Her smile slipped a little. "One copes as best one can."

Kitty gave her an understanding smile. "Friendships can often be more rewarding than family ties."

"I quite agree." Stephanie gave Juliet a sidelong glance. "When Cody marries Juliet, however, I'll be gaining a most amiable sister."

Kitty and Prudence both exclaimed, "What!" so loudly that the dogs' ears rose.

"I thought you knew!" Stephanie's eyes widened. "If I spoke out of turn, I'm so sorry!"

Inwardly, Juliet winced. She hadn't mentioned the engagement ruse to her sister in her letters because she'd wanted to explain it in person. Until she could confide the truth to Kitty in private, however, she was forced to play along.

"Ah…yes. Cody Gryphon proposed and I accepted."

Kitty's jaw dropped. "Tell me everything!"

"Well…I first saw Cody at Lord and Lady Ayscoghe's soirée and I thought for a moment my heart had stopped."

Stephanie giggled. "The night of the soirée, Cody told me he felt the same thing about you."

Juliet's face warmed. "Did he?"

Her sister's eyes twinkled. "Is he handsome?"

"I-I've never seen any man who appealed to me more. Both Mama and Papa are well pleased at the match."

"What an auspicious sign! I've never known the two of them to agree on much of anything." Kitty laughed. "Once you're settled in, I'll press you for more details."

"You've come to Grovebrook a little early, I'm afraid," Prudence said. "There's to be a harvest festival in October which should be a great deal of fun, but perhaps you can come back then. We'll all be pitching in to make decorations."

Prudence began to talk about all the wonderful food to be had at the festival, including freshly-pressed apple cider from the grove adjacent to her cottage. Although she feigned interest, Juliet was preoccupied with her cool parting from Cody that morning. Even though he despised her, she couldn't help but wish they were still friends. In addition, she wondered whether his cousin had decided to do anything about Violet. Unfortunately, with so many people around, she'd had no opportunity to inquire.

Suddenly, she realized her sister had asked her a question. "I'm sorry, what did you say?"

"Daydreaming of a certain gentleman? I believe I was just as easily distracted when I first fell in love with Philip." Kitty laughed. "At any rate, I was asking if you'd like to see the town? We're driving through now."

Juliet glanced out the window to see a pristine little village, filled with well-kept shops and businesses. "How charming!"

"Philip says Grovebrook was quite neglected when he arrived. He had to do a great deal to the place to make it presentable."

"The residents tell me all the time how much better things are since Philip purchased the place," Prudence said. "Apparently, Lord Moregate's former representative was dreadfully dishonest and unpleasant besides."

"How is Lord Kirkham enjoying managing the town?" Juliet asked.

"Actually Freddie adores working, much more than he anticipated. He says his duties give him a sense of satisfaction at the end of the day, and he likes being a help to Philip. As for me, I enjoy socializing with the townspeople. In my former life as a hothouse flower, I wouldn't have been afforded the opportunity to do so." She pointed at a house as they drove by. "That's where

Freddie and I live, at Cousin's Cottage. I'm able to spin wool and knit lace to my heart's content, with nobody to criticize!"

Prudence's happiness was catching, and Juliet found her dour mood dissipating.

"I'm looking forward to our visit very much. London is exciting, to be sure, but the constant scrutiny can be stifling."

"And the gossip!" Stephanie shook her head. "That's the problem with society; nobody has anything worthwhile to do, so they pay far too much attention to other people's business."

Kitty gave Prudence an amused glance before making a response. "You've put your finger on it, exactly, Miss Gryphon."

"Do call me Stephanie, Lady Philip. We're so far from London, I wouldn't want to stand on ceremony."

"Thank you, Stephanie. Please call me Kitty, then."

Prudence waved. "And I'm Prudence."

The carriage turned onto a driveway, and the manor house was revealed.

"Oh, Kitty, your home is perfectly lovely!" Juliet beamed. "I can't wait to see inside."

Augustus was shocked when Philip arrived at the London townhouse in the late afternoon, but he shook his younger brother's hand with pleasure. "You're the last person I expected to see, especially since Juliet is on her way to Grovebrook with Miss Gryphon. Are you in town long?"

"Hopefully not. Is Father here with you?"

Augustus peered at Philip, whose face was etched with worry. "He just left for the club for drinks and an early dinner with Miss Gryphon's father, Lord Horatio. Is something amiss?"

"Juliet's letter to Kitty this morning was the first I'd heard about Father's supposed financial difficulty. I came as quickly as

I could, but I don't understand why either of you didn't let me know sooner."

"We thought it best not to worry you. Father has a new man of business now, and he's approved a list of economies. Most significantly, however, Father has arranged my marriage to Miss Gryphon. The wealth she brings to the match will buoy our assets until we're in the black once more."

"What about Juliet?"

"She and I were taken aback by the news, admittedly, but we've adjusted to the realities of the situation tolerably well."

Philip made a sound of frustration. "Have you already proposed to Miss Gryphon?"

"Not yet. Not officially, anyway. I decided to wait a few more days so we can get better acquainted."

"Well, you needn't propose to her at all. The estate is perfectly sound."

"I'm afraid it's not." Augustus frowned. "I examined the books personally, Philip. Meadow's End is losing money every month."

"As you very well know, I was poring over the books for months before Father agreed to sell Grovebrook to me. Although I heartily concur that economies should be made, those records don't reflect the entirety of Father's wealth."

"What? I'm not following you."

"Mother brought assets to the marriage, including shares in coal-gas companies. The dividends from those leases are paid annually into a separate bank account, and then the cash is made available for the running of Meadow's End. Didn't Mr. Randall bring that account to your attention?"

"No." Augustus felt slightly dizzy and he was obliged to sit down. "Father discharged Randall in favor of a new man-of-business, Mr. Burton Kelly. None of us discovered the existence of this other account. Are you quite certain of your information?"

"There's a ledger detailing the account at the bottom of the safe, underneath Mother's jewels. I suspect if Randall was discharged, he failed to disclose its existence to Father out of spite. Even so, Mother should have told you. Randall always reviewed the account with her annually."

"Since she doesn't know about the financial difficulty, she'd no reason to mention the account. Father didn't want say anything to her until we'd sorted out the emergency."

"Merciful heavens, Augustus! You almost ruined your life by rushing into marriage with the wrong woman!" Philip scratched his head. "Here's what we'll do: get your hat and we'll go to the bank right now. You need to see the account balance for yourself. Then, we'll go to the club to have a word with Father and Lord Horatio. This arranged marriage is wholly unnecessary."

MILES APART

At a private table in his Pall Mall gentlemen's club, Lord Moregate examined the statement Augustus brought from the bank. "So it seems we're not so ruined after all." He glanced up, stricken. "I don't know whether to be relieved or angry with myself. If I'd taken a stronger interest in the management of our affairs from the beginning, I never would have overlooked this."

Lord Horatio peered at him. "I'm glad for you, Moregate, but where does this leave my daughter? We had an agreement."

Augustus cleared his throat. "Miss Gryphon should be told the facts, of course, so she feels no obligation. That being said, I should still like to pursue her."

Philip cocked his head. "You would? We all believed you and Juliet—"

"Juliet and I discussed the matter and we both agreed we would be better off as friends. She'll not be injured by me as a result of this new development, but I can't say the same for her and Mr. Gryphon."

Horatio raised an eyebrow. "So you're aware of the ruse?"

"Indeed, I am. I didn't realize it had been brought to your attention, but I'm glad you know."

"Ruse?" Philip echoed. "To what ruse might you be referring?"

"I confess, I'm in the dark as well," Moregate said.

"To allay any gossip about a romantic relationship between Juliet and myself, she and Mr. Gryphon agreed to enter into a temporary engagement."

"You're joking!" Philip looked aghast.

"Not at all." Augustus frowned. "It pains me to say so, but it would be helpful to me if they continued the ruse until Miss Gryphon is truly convinced of my regard for her."

"Since Cody wishes to see his sister happy, I'm sure that won't be a problem. I'll speak to him tonight," Horatio replied. "Due to the fact Miss Beaucroft is no longer in town, however, there's very little opportunity for her and Cody to interact."

"I'm leaving for Grovebrook the day after tomorrow. Perhaps Mr. Gryphon would like to come along?" Augustus asked. "He may best demonstrate his supposed zeal for Juliet if he's under the same roof."

Philip shook his head. "Mr. Gryphon is more than welcome, of course, but I can't help but be concerned about Juliet's feelings on the matter."

Augustus chuckled. "In truth, I've noticed a marked attraction between Juliet and Mr. Gryphon. I, for one, should like to see it unfold."

"I agree," Horatio said. "I suspect Cody cares more for Miss Beaucroft than he has yet to admit to himself."

Philip groaned. "Romantic ruses can be dangerous ploys."

Augustus gave his brother a sidelong glance. "And yet sometimes they work out for the best, do they not?"

"True." He sighed. "When I return to Grovebrook tomorrow, I'll inform Kitty of the situation privately. I'll also announce that we are to expect a visit from both Mr. Gryphon and Augustus.

Anything more than that, Augustus may address when he arrives."

"Yes, I'd prefer to discuss the situation with Miss Gryphon myself." He frowned. "I hope she welcomes my courtship, otherwise Mr. Gryphon and I will be returning to London on the next train."

~

LADY LOVEJOY WAS DINING out that evening, and Lord Horatio had gone to his club, so Cody ate a solitary meal and then retired to his room with a book. As he read, however, his eyes kept wandering from the page. Juliet's frosty demeanor at the train station had apparently bothered him more than he realized, if his lack of concentration was the measure. He thought back to their argument, wishing he could have handled it differently. His manner had been high-handed and he ought to apologize—but should he? Perhaps he ought to leave things the way they were. If Juliet viewed him as a villain, she could more easily turn her attention to another gentleman. No doubt Mr. Waters would be delighted to step into his shoes as her next fiancé.

He stared at a spot on the carpet, scowling. Waters was a bumbling fool and an idiot who could never make Juliet happy. Surely she'd never welcome the attentions of a man whose ears stuck out on either side of his head and whose chin was nowhere to be found. Of course, she might accept the man out of desperation, if society gossips made too much out of her broken engagement. Indeed, he might be morally responsible for driving her into the arms of all manner of reprobates. The notion of Juliet sitting on another man's lap made him clench his fists with fury. Why couldn't he forget about that night in the library, and why should he care whom she married?

A tap on his door interrupted his gloomy reverie. He opened the door to discover his father in the hallway with his hat in hand and a cape draped over one arm. Cody concluded he'd just arrived from the club.

"Might I have a word, lad?"

"Of course." Cody ushered him inside the room.

Horatio sighed as he sank down into a chair. "What a night."

"How was your dinner with Lord Moregate?"

His father frowned. "There's been a little wrinkle in my quest to marry Stephanie to Lord Elbourne. It seems Moregate is *not* in financial distress after all and his son's marriage to an heiress is no longer a necessity."

"What?"

Just as Cody was poised to let loose a stream of ungentlemanly invectives, his father held up a quelling hand. "Despite that, he's professed his desire to woo Stephanie."

Cody's shoulders relaxed. "I should hope so!"

"To that end, he's requested you continue your ruse with Miss Beaucroft for the time being."

"How am I to do that, exactly, when we're miles apart?"

"You're to travel with him to Grovebrook the day after tomorrow, for an extended visit."

Cody groaned. "Miss Beaucroft despises me! We had a quarrel yesterday afternoon and never mended it. Once we're together again, I very much doubt our ruse will appear believable to anyone."

"I suggest you find a way to ingratiate yourself with the girl. Surely it won't be too much of a hardship?"

Something stirred deep inside Cody at the thought of holding Juliet in his arms again. Although there was no future in it, he very much wished to smooth things over. He gave his father a nod. "No, sir. It will pose no hardship whatsoever."

～

AFTER A FESTIVE DINNER at Constance Hall, which Prudence and Lord Kirkham attended, the small party moved into the drawing room for a little entertainment. Juliet and Prudence played the piano, Kitty and Kirkham sang a duet, and Stephanie applauded madly after each performance. Juliet tried to encourage her friend to perform, to no avail.

"Do you sing or play, Stephanie?"

"I'm afraid my skills are more the sporting variety. Archery, riding, and billiards are my favorites. I can also shoot."

Kirkham brightened. "Shotguns?"

"Pistols, mainly. When we were in Texas, Cody and I used to line up bottles on a split-post fence and shoot the bottles off. I became rather good at it." She laughed. "Once, when we were walking through some brush, Cody frightened a rattlesnake. I shot it when it was about three inches from his boot and he said he wasn't certain which had made him more nervous—the snake or my marksmanship."

Prudence's eyes widened. "I dislike snakes so much I'm sure I would have been perfectly useless! Your cool nerves and steady hand are much to be admired."

Stephanie giggled. "I'm worthy of admiration in Texas, perhaps, but not here. Lady Lovejoy held Juliet up to me as the perfect model of decorum, and I quite agree."

Perfect model of decorum? As Juliet remembered asking Cody to ruin her, she flushed with embarrassment. If the countess had known she was capable of such a proposition, she would never have introduced Stephanie to her at all!

After Prudence and Kirkham said their reluctant good-byes, it was time to retire. As Juliet readied herself for bed, Kitty slipped into her room, candle in hand, and shut the door behind her. She was clad in her dressing gown and her long dark hair hung down her back in a mass of curls. Even in such casual disarray, with her hair unbound, Juliet thought her sister was extraordinarily beautiful. Unfortunately, she was also shrewd.

"Now, Juliet, I can tell you're hiding something."

"You can?"

Kitty nodded. "Between the two of us you're far more level-headed, so your sudden engagement makes no sense at all. I'm convinced there's another explanation entirely, and I won't leave until you tell me what it is."

"You know me all too well, I'm afraid."

Her sister put down the candle, picked up the hair brush, and began to brush Juliet's hair, just as she had when they were little. In a rush, Juliet told her the series of events leading up to the supposed engagement—omitting the humiliating scene in the library, of course.

Kitty stared at her. "I can't believe after everything that happened to me this Season, you'd resort to a ruse."

"Don't scold me. I was desperate."

"I'm not taking you to task. It's just that I'm worried for you." Kitty studied her. "So your heart isn't broken where Augustus is concerned?"

"I admit it was difficult to accept at first, but only because I'd grown so used to the idea of being his wife. After I met Cody Gryphon, however, I realized there was a different aspect to romance I'd never felt before. Forgive me if this seems coarse or vulgar, but there was a more physical element I hadn't anticipated."

"But I thought you said your relationship with Mr. Gryphon is a ruse?"

"The engagement is a ruse, but my feelings for him are genuine…I think."

"Does your heart race when he's near?"

"Yes."

"Does he give you tingles all the way down your spine and out to your fingertips?"

"Oh, yes."

"Do you experience a melting sensation inside when you think of him?"

"Yes, along with the most scandalous thoughts." Juliet nodded. "Then you know exactly how I feel."

"I understand perfectly. And such physical attraction is worth having in a marriage, if you can manage it."

With a long sigh, Juliet pulled her hair over one shoulder and began to twist it into a braid. "I'm attracted to Cody, but we'll never be married. Not only does he intend to return to Texas, but he and I quarreled. I think he detests me now."

Kitty perched at the foot of her bed. "Might I ask the subject of the disagreement?"

Inwardly, Juliet winced. How could she describe the argument without giving too much away? "I-It was a theoretical discussion about how to treat a former friend who has wronged you or someone you love. If such a person asks for your help, with nowhere else to turn, what moral obligation do you have?"

"Hmm…that's a difficult question to answer without a specific example to go on."

Juliet pretended to think. "Um…well, let's say someone like Violet Haver had sent a letter, begging for help. Just to make it worse, let's say she'd been cast off by her family, was living with an elderly aunt, and was…in a family way. She wants you to contact Lord Gryphon and beg him to marry her. What would you do?"

"How ghastly. I expect my first response would be to toss the letter in the fireplace and forget she ever existed."

"That's what I said, but Cody thought me horribly unfeeling."

"He doesn't know you well at all to reach such a conclusion."

"No, he doesn't."

"At any rate, if I pushed my resentment of her behavior aside and tried to view Violet as I would a complete stranger, my response might change a little. Under no circumstances would I speak with Lord Gryphon, of course, but I'd have to consider what sort of charity to extend to a desperate woman in need." She shook her head. "One must always be careful about taking on other people's problems, especially with a girl like Violet. Strict limits are required, or she'd always be asking for more." She paused. "When did she send you this letter?"

Juliet felt at once miserable and relieved her sister knew the truth. "Several days ago. Violet's living in Little Brambleton with a distant relative. I showed her letter to Cody, who then brought it to his cousin. He hoped to talk some sense into the man, but I don't know if he succeeded or not. Nevertheless, I thought perhaps she could use money."

"I'm certain she could, but if she's to support herself and a baby, what she really needs is an honest trade. I expect Prudence would go with you to Little Brambleton, if you asked. She's awfully clever with her hands, and might have some good advice."

"Prudence is the daughter of an earl. Don't you suppose she'd consider such a task beneath her?"

"She's never stood on ceremony, even before her marriage to Freddie. Why don't you visit Cousin's Cottage tomorrow to arrange it?"

"I can't let Stephanie know what I'm doing."

"Hmm. In that case, perhaps we should wait until Augustus arrives. Once he's here, she'll not want to leave his side, I'm sure." Kitty cocked her head. "I'm curious why you haven't confided in your friend? She doesn't seem the sort to shrink from the realities of human frailty."

"At first, I said nothing because I didn't want to trespass on Violet's privacy. Now, I don't want Cody to find out. He'd think the only reason I went to help is because he shamed me into it."

Kitty's eyebrows rose. "If Mr. Gryphon is truly that petty, I'm afraid I must agree with you. You and he will never marry."

She slid off the bed and kissed Juliet on the forehead. "Please don't ever be afraid to confide in me."

"Thank you. You're the best friend anyone could ever have."

As her sister left, Juliet blinked back tears. Was Cody indeed petty or was her assessment of his character unfair? With the awkwardness between them, she'd probably never know.

CODY SETTLED himself in the seat opposite Augustus and shortly thereafter the train began to move. The private compartment was roomy and comfortable, which made the hours-long journey somewhat bearable. Nevertheless, Cody had a fleeting wish he could stay put somewhere for a little while. Nearly three months had passed since he left America, and he was beginning to find non-stop touring somewhat tiresome.

The earl caught his eye and nodded. "Thank you for coming with me to Grovebrook. It's an extraordinarily selfish thing for me to ask, but your presence will reassure Miss Gryphon when I tell her the contract of marriage has been canceled."

"You mean to say she won't leap to conclusions as far as Juliet is concerned?"

Augustus chuckled. "Just so."

"And what of Juliet's feelings? You don't suppose her hopes will be unfairly raised at the news you needn't marry wealth after all?"

"She and I have settled matters between us."

Cody frowned. "You could have any woman you choose, and yet you chose Stephanie. Please don't misunderstand; I think my sister is a tremendous girl and I love her dearly, but she's just so completely different than the other debutantes."

"Those differences are what recommend her so highly." Augustus smiled. "I find Miss Gryphon's spirit refreshing. Until we met, I didn't realize how much I'd respond to a lady like her."

"I'll take your word for it."

Augustus studied him. "You still intend to return to Texas?"

"I do. Father sold his cattle ranch, but I purchased land for myself. Four hundred acres of prime property, with a stream. I intend to harvest timber and farm cattle." He shrugged. "After Texas joins the Union, I might even run for office."

"How different we are, Gryphon! I yearn for the exotic, and you wax nostalgic for the familiar." He paused. "If it's the life of a gentleman farmer you crave, you can obtain that in England. You remind me of Philip, in a way. He wouldn't rest until he became a landowner."

"I can't say that I blame him." Cody gazed out the window. "In Texas, a man can be anything or anyone he wants to be, without worrying about heritage. A man without a title can create his own empire, with a little luck and hard work." He grinned. "And the girls are very pretty, too. One can have one's pick of *señoritas* or Texas belles."

"You make it sound rather appealing."

"It's not the sort of place for a nobleman like you, of course, but it suits me rather well."

"If that's the case, I beg you not to trifle with Juliet's affections."

"Ha! Both you and Stephanie have accused me of the same thing, but your concerns are for naught. Although we'll act the loving couple for my sister's benefit, Juliet and I are estranged." Cody tried to keep a frown from his face, but his muscles tensed all the same. "I'll do my best to ameliorate the situation, but I imagine she could never feel anything romantic for me."

"Perhaps it's best to keep it that way."

Cody nodded, but he fell silent thereafter. He was to spend several days in the same house as Juliet and make no effort to caress her face or kiss her lips? A worse torture was never devised.

~

Toward the end of breakfast, Phillip folded his napkin by his plate, rose, and bent to give Kitty a kiss on the cheek. "I'm off to meet Kirkham about the harvest festival."

"Problems?"

"Just a few logistical issues to work out." He gave Juliet and Stephanie a smile. "Don't forget, we've two additional guests to welcome this afternoon. I'll be back before then."

Stephanie giggled. "I can't wait to see Augustus. And for your sake, Juliet, I'm so glad Cody could come along."

"It's a wonderful turn of events."

As Juliet slid a surreptitious glance toward her sister, Kitty covered a smile with her napkin. When Philip had returned from London the day before, he'd spoken to them both about the demise of the arranged marriage between Augustus and Stephanie. Although Juliet was well aware she and Cody were to resume their ruse, she wondered if he would find it too distasteful to bear. Should worse come to worst, she could always announce she'd broken their engagement. If Cody wasn't forced to pretend affection for her, perhaps he'd be more civil.

"Stephanie, shall we practice 'Sleeping, I Dreamed Love' after breakfast?" Juliet asked.

"Oh, yes, please do," Kitty urged. "I'd like to have a salon tonight."

Stephanie wrinkled her nose. "Are you absolutely sure I won't make a fool of myself? I've never sung for anyone before."

"With a little more practice, you'll perform beautifully."

Kitty nodded. "I couldn't help but overhear you singing yesterday, Stephanie, and I thought you did well."

Juliet nodded. "Just think how surprised and pleased Augustus will be at your performance."

"All right. Mercifully, the lyrics are short." Stephanie sighed. "I'll practice for an hour, but then I'd like to ride."

"What a wonderful idea! I could use the exercise. Kitty, would care to join us?"

"Why not? I haven't been on a horse since I arrived in Grovebrook."

"Here's an idea; let's practice our song later and go riding now." Stephanie's face shone with excitement.

Juliet gave her sister a quizzical glance, and Kitty responded with a smile. "Let's visit Prudence. It's a bit early to be paying calls, but she always loves company."

A half hour later, the three ladies had donned riding habits and were guiding their mounts down the driveway. The route to town was edged on either side by burgeoning fields of wheat.

"Just seeing all these crops reminds me of making corn husk dolls back home," Stephanie said.

Juliet and Kitty exchanged a puzzled glance.

"What are those?" Juliet asked.

"Oh, Indian women use husks and thread to fashion dolls. One of the squaws showed me how to do it when I was a little girl.

Kitty gave her a startled glance. "Indians?"

Stephanie laughed. "Our ranch was in the southeastern part of Texas and didn't encroach on Comanche territory, so they didn't bother us. In fact, many Texian ranchers took women of Indian descent for brides." She glanced at Kitty. "Speaking of territory, does all this land belong to Lord Philip?"

"Yes, but most of it is let to tenants. A sheep farm is located about a half-mile from here and there's also a vineyard on the far side of town. An apiary is located adjacent to the vineyard. The tenant—Mr. Atkins—will have a booth at the festival to sell honey and candles. We'll be sure to purchase large quantities of each for Constance Hall."

Stephanie took in a deep breath of fresh air. "Cody will love it here in the country."

Her statement piqued Juliet's curiosity. "Is Grovebrook anything like Texas?"

"Not especially, but it's far more picturesque and varied. In parts of Texas, you can ride for days and never see any living creatures but birds and prairie dogs."

"Or snakes." Kitty giggled. "I've never seen Prudence go so pale when you mentioned snakes after dinner the other night."

"I don't mean to pry, but Prudence mentioned an estrangement with her father." Stephanie frowned. "I feel very sorry for her."

"Lord Trestlebury couldn't accept her marriage to Lord Kirkham, I'm afraid," Kitty said.

"But Lord Kirkham is excellent company and exceedingly amiable! I can't imagine anyone finding fault with him."

"Yes, but he's also a viscount without any sort of fortune. Lord Trestlebury felt it was a tremendous comedown for Prudence and turned his back on them both. Fortunately, Lady Trestlebury is thrilled with her son-in-law. She's been to visit several times, on her own."

"It hurts my heart to think Prudence's father could be so cold and unfeeling."

Having recently been accused of the same flaw, Juliet felt compelled to argue the point.

"I don't agree with Lord Trestlebury's decision, but you must look at the situation from his perspective. Prudence is his only daughter, and he wanted her to marry well. I have the feeling the man overreacted to her elopement and now doesn't know how to mend the fence."

Kitty nodded. "You could be right, Juliet, but Philip informs me that Lord Trestlebury is quite rigid in his thinking. It will take a miracle to change his mind."

IVY

Juliet, Stephanie, and Kitty settled into Prudence's cozy parlor, where the chairs were draped with white doilies. A knitting basket on the floor was heaped with an afghan-in-progress, and a large spinning wheel sat in the corner. Stephanie was particularly enchanted with the graceful device. "You can spin? You must show me how to do it sometime during my visit."

"I'd be more than happy to show you. I find spinning to be extremely relaxing."

Kitty peered at Prudence, concern etched on her features. "You're most awfully pale."

Juliet had also noticed the bloom on Prudence's cheeks was absent. "Are you unwell? Perhaps you ought to go lie down."

"I may have eaten something that disagreed with me, but I can't decide what it may have been. Since the upset comes and goes, I'm entirely uncertain." A brief smile reached her lips. "I actually made poor Freddie sleep in the guest room last night so I could get some rest, but it didn't help."

Kitty rose. "Shall I ask Nettie to bring you a cup of tea?"

A nod. "Thank you, yes. Tea is the only thing I've managed to keep down this morning."

As Kitty hastened from the room to go in search of the cook/housekeeper, Stephanie gave Prudence a sympathetic smile.

"I'm so sorry we bothered you. It's entirely my fault since I insisted on riding to town."

Prudence shut her eyes for a long moment and pressed a handkerchief to her mouth. When the wave of nausea passed, she breathed a sigh of relief. "I'm glad you've come, actually. It gives me something to concentrate on other than the location of the chamber pot."

Kitty returned. "The tea is on its way."

"Thank you."

"How long have you been married, Prudence?" Stephanie asked.

"Oh, I suppose it's been over six weeks now." She managed a giggle. "Seems like it was just yesterday."

Stephanie cleared her throat. "Forgive me for being blunt, but have your courses been regular?"

Prudence's eyes widened. "I haven't thought about it." She frowned as she pondered the matter. "I've not been bothered with them since the wedding." A flash of fear crossed her face. "Do you suppose that means there's something terribly wrong with me?"

"No, not in the least." Stephanie gave Kitty a wry smile. "Do you have a midwife in Grovebrook? I expect you'll have need of one in another eight months or so."

If the Texian had suddenly performed a magic trick, the room could not have been more astonished. Juliet and Kitty both gasped in surprise. Prudence peered at Stephanie, shock clearly registering on her pretty features.

"But it's too soon for something like that!"

"Not at all." She giggled. "In matters such as these, I'm far less sheltered than most girls my age. In Texas, the ladies banded together and shared all sorts of information that might make you blush. I think it quite likely you're to have a baby by early spring."

Prudence's hand dropped to her tummy, as if by doing so she could somehow discern the possible life within. "I-I couldn't possibly be that fortunate, could I? Freddie will faint! Oh, but I mustn't say anything to him until I'm absolutely certain. You must all promise to do the same."

"Since it's your secret to tell, we'll all keep your confidence," Kitty said.

Juliet nodded. "I wouldn't dream of spoiling your surprise."

"Things should become more obvious in a month or two," Stephanie said. "Fortunately, feeling ill usually passes after three months."

The tea arrived then, and the three ladies fussed over Prudence, fetching a footstool for her feet and a pillow to cushion her chair. By the time they said their good-byes, Juliet was pleased to see a little color had returned to the woman's face.

As Juliet rode back to Constance Hall with Stephanie and Kitty, her admiration for the Texian had risen even higher than before.

"Stephanie, you don't shrink from things which would give most girls the vapors," Juliet said. "I'm rather in awe."

She waved away the compliment. "Thank you, but it's just a reflection of my upbringing. I've even seen cows and horses give birth, so there's not much that disturbs me anymore."

Kitty giggled. "Grandmama frightened me so much about marriage on the eve of my wedding, I had nightmares. I'm happy to report she was wrong." She glanced at Juliet and Stephanie. "Love does indeed conquer all."

Juliet smiled, but fell silent thereafter. Love might conquer all, but why did it have to be so complicated? She'd believed herself to be in love with Augustus, but Cody had proved otherwise. Now she found herself infatuated with a man who both disdained her character and couldn't wait to depart from England. Would she ever meet another man who excited her in the way he did, or was she destined to settle for a merely comfortable fit? Certainly, none of the gentlemen she'd met this past Season had stirred her senses whatsoever.

Her hands tightened on the reins as she realized Prudence's good news meant a more pressing problem had arisen. The fortunate lady might still be willing to accompany her to Little Brambleton, but Juliet didn't have the heart to ask. In her current condition, the motion of the train might upset her stomach and the whole journey would be a disaster. How was she to visit Violet now? With houseguests to care for, Kitty was altogether too busy to leave Grovebrook. Juliet sighed. Even though the presence of an unchaperoned girl might raise the eyebrows of fellow travelers, she'd just have to manage the excursion alone.

As CODY STEPPED from the hired carriage, he viewed Constance Hall with approbation. In fact, after he and Augustus had departed the Grovebrook rail station, very little had met with his disapproval. He'd enjoyed driving through the cheerful well-kept village, with its quaint architecture and friendly faces. In addition, the sight of flourishing fruit trees and crops gave the place a sense of prosperity and made him glad he'd come.

"Why, Constance Hall is utterly charming! And it's quite a manageable distance from the train station."

Augustus nodded. "Yes, everything I've seen reflects creditably on Philip. I'm impressed."

People began pouring from the house, from the butler and servants, to Philip, Kitty, Stephanie, and Juliet. Cody bowed to

Philip, who introduced him to Juliet's sister. Although Cody thought the woman was absolutely stunning, Juliet's delicate bone structure and large, expressive blue eyes made him yearn to carry her off to a flower-laden bower where they could be alone. He'd been a fool for taking her to task the way he had, and he had no explanation for it.

"Hello, *querida*. I'm very glad to see you."

"And I'm glad to see you."

The rote recitation of greetings was for his sister's benefit, but the exchange fell far short of genuine sentiment. Would Stephanie wonder why the spark between him and Juliet was so restrained? When Cody bent to deposit a kiss on Juliet's soft cheek, he was surprised she tilted her face to receive the gentle caress with seeming pleasure. Either she was a very good actress, or her attraction to him had not completely vanished. His eyes dropped to her luscious mouth, but he dared not risk stealing a genuine kiss. Juliet would undoubtedly slap his face in response and Augustus would probably thrash him afterward. His visit would certainly not be off to a good start.

He didn't realize he was staring at Juliet until Stephanie gave his arm a squeeze.

"Cody, you're looking at your fiancée as if you were starving wolf and she were a tender rabbit. Behave yourself."

"Oh, forgive me." Cody felt his cheekbones burn, and he tried to cover his embarrassment with a joke. "Juliet does look delectable, however, and I'm longing for some tea."

Philip laughed. "You've arrived just in time then. Let's go inside and I'll have it brought around."

STEPHANIE LINKED her arm with Juliet's on the way to the drawing room, and bent her head closer to whisper, "I noticed your quarrel with my brother was quickly forgotten!" She giggled. "He's never been as enraptured with any girl as he is with you."

"I suppose we're so glad to be reunited, our disagreement has been pushed aside for now."

"I'll hope it stays that way."

Stephanie sank into a chair, and Juliet settled herself onto the horsehair sofa. When Cody sat down by her side, waves of pleasure coursed through her body. How could the man be so despicably handsome? He'd woven a spell like some sort of warlock, and she felt irresistibly drawn to him. It was only by an extreme act of will she hadn't met his lips with hers in the courtyard.

Augustus and Cody chatted about the journey, but Juliet was so preoccupied by her wicked thoughts that she scarcely paid any attention to what was being said. After the tea tray arrived, she nibbled on a slice of freshly-baked lemon cake, which was at once tart and sweet. A large crumb fell into her lap, and before she could react, Cody reached out to pick it up.

"Allow me." His fingers hovered near her mouth until her lips parted, then he put the crumb on her tongue. "Can't have something so delicious go to waste, can we?"

"No," she managed.

When her eyes met his, she saw the fire within them. Hers were apparently not the only wicked thoughts accompanying the tea! She averted her gaze, reminding herself how much she resented the man who called himself her fiancé. No wonder Stephanie had warned her away from Cody; he really was a wolf.

Augustus put down his teacup. "I have news of some significance which you all ought to hear." He produced a beautiful ring and held it up. "I brought this ring of engagement with me as a token of my intentions. Miss Gryphon, I came to Constance Hall with the intent to woo you, even though the necessity for our union no longer exists."

"No longer exists?" Stephanie echoed. "I don't follow your meaning."

"My father's estate isn't in financial jeopardy and never was, as it turns out." He nodded toward his brother. "Thanks to Philip, we uncovered a critical asset we'd overlooked. My father and Lord Horatio have agreed to cancel our contract of marriage, and you're now under no obligation to accept me. Nevertheless, with your permission, I'd like the opportunity to court you properly."

Stephanie glanced at Juliet, as if gauging her reaction. Instinctively, Juliet knew if she showed the slightest hesitation or dismay, her friend would be terribly hurt.

"What a fortuitous circumstance! I'm so pleased for you, Stephanie." Juliet reached for Cody's hand. "You deserve to fall in love, just like your brother and I have."

"I quite agree." Cody brought Juliet's hand to his lips.

"I'm not asking for your answer to my proposal just yet, Miss Gryphon." Augustus slid the ring into his pocket. "When you say yes, I want you to be absolutely sure."

"If that's the case, I won't give you my answer right now." She smiled. "But you do have my permission to court me."

The tense muscles around Augustus's mouth eased, and Kitty and Philip breathed a visible sigh of relief.

"Well, all things considered, I think a bit of sherry is in order." Philip rang for a servant. "I feel like celebrating."

Augustus's delighted expression made him look almost boyish. "Hear, hear."

When the sherry arrived, the servant handed glasses all around.

"Here's to courtship." Cody lifted his glass by way of a toast and took a sip.

"To courtship," everyone answered.

As Juliet drank her toast, she noticed Augustus give Stephanie a beaming smile. A wistful feeling slid down her throat along with the sweet wine. Oh, what she wouldn't give to have Cody pursue her the same way.

❥

AFTER TEA, Philip offered to show Augustus and Cody the stables, and Kitty excused herself to confer with the cook about dinner. At loose ends, Juliet and Stephanie brought their dogs outside to a hedged-in side yard so the animals could play. As the pups tussled and chased one another across the velvety grass, Stephanie gave a contented sigh.

"I'm so very glad you're in love with my brother. Otherwise, when Lord Elbourne told me the arrangement between us had been canceled, I would have thought he meant to throw me over in your favor."

"You're joking, of course."

"Yes, I'm teasing. Obviously, everyone can see how you and my brother are with one another. The way he regards you is almost scandalous!"

"I confess, I enjoy it." Juliet's words rang true. Even though she was aware Cody was feigning his admiration, it was easy to get caught up in the pretense. The trick was to avoid being ensnared in it.

"Lord Kirkham behaves the same infatuated way with Prudence, and Lord Philip acts as if there is no other woman in the world when Kitty is near." Stephanie's eyes sparkled. "I was ready to accept Lord Elbourne's proposal, if he offered one. Now, however, I'm looking forward to the courtship. Out here in the country, nobody will disapprove of our little flirtations or gossip about our tête-à-têtes."

The rapidly approaching pounding of horses' hooves drew their attention. As they gazed out over the low hedge, Cody, Philip, and Augustus streaked past on horseback, with Cody in the lead.

Juliet gave Stephanie an excited glance. "It seems the gentlemen are racing. Shall we watch?"

"Oh, yes." Stephanie scooped up her puppy. "If I can't race alongside, watching is the next best thing."

Juliet retrieved Robin Hood and settled him in her arms. "There's a break in the hedge just over here."

They hastened over to the opening, but the horses were almost out of sight. Stephanie craned her neck. "Wait...they're coming back!"

Indeed, the gentlemen had circled their mounts around and were speeding back the way they'd come. Divots of earth flew in the wake of the horses' passage, and Juliet felt her pulse quicken with excitement. As the racers approached, Cody was several lengths ahead. He veered off to the side a little way so he could jump over a narrow gully. The jump scarcely slowed him down at all, and in fact Cody was still in the lead when he landed on the other side.

"Well done," she murmured.

Once the gentlemen had reached whatever landmark had been agreed upon, the contest was over. Judging from the laughter echoing across the field, the trio had enjoyed the exercise. Juliet's eyebrows rose when Cody began to demonstrate a riding maneuver.

"What's he doing?"

"It's a figure eight. Cody learned all sorts of riding and roping tricks from Mexican *vaqueros*. He's really very good."

Although Juliet admired the man's prowess, she felt crestfallen. Cody's life in Texas was certainly packed with more excitement and adventure than he could ever hope to find with her. If she'd ever harbored a secret hope he might change his mind about leaving, she'd just been disabused of the notion.

Just then, she heard Kitty calling her name. When Juliet and Stephanie returned to the side yard, her sister wore a strained expression.

"There you are! A message from Grandmama was delivered just now. We're to expect her for dinner."

"H-How lovely." Despite Juliet's response, a wave of panic swept over her. The last person she could expect to fool with a ruse would be Ivy Beaucroft. "This will be a perfect opportunity to tell her about my engagement."

Kitty's eyes registered unspoken sympathy. "She'll be terribly interested in all the details."

Undue interest from Ivy was exactly what Juliet feared most. "I imagine so."

"I've extended Grandmama invitations to dine before, but she's never decided to come until now. I suspect she's heard we have company."

"It's my fault, I'm sure of it. I wrote her a letter before I left London and told her of my impending visit."

Stephanie lit up. "I'm to meet your grandmama? I'm so looking forward to it."

"Yes." Juliet forced a smile to her lips. "It should be an exciting evening."

ALTHOUGH IVY BEAUCROFT was in possession of no title, she sailed into the drawing room like a countess. Kitty and Juliet each bestowed a kiss on her cheek, which she received with pleasure. Augustus and Philip also greeted the older woman warmly, after which Kitty introduced the Gryphons.

Ivy peered first at Stephanie. "You're quite pretty for an American girl."

"Thank you, but actually I was born in England. Nevertheless, I rather consider myself a Texian."

Ivy's eyes narrowed with disapproval. "Hmm. I suppose it can't be helped." Her attention turned to Cody. "Merciful heavens but you look remarkably like Lord Gryphon!" She glanced at Juliet. "You didn't mention *that* in your letters."

"Actually, I hardly notice the resemblance any longer." Juliet took a deep breath. "Mr. Gryphon and I are engaged."

"Oh?" Ivy's eyebrows rose and she slid Juliet a severe glance. "I can't wait to hear all about your courtship and what led up to your happy betrothal. I feel certain it will be a fascinating tale."

"Perhaps we'll chat about it after dinner."

"The anticipation will be unbearable."

Cody bowed. "I hope my manners are more gentlemanly than those of my cousin, Mrs. Beaucroft."

"I trust they will be." She cocked her head. "Your accent is muddy, but distinctly English."

"I was born in Gloucester, and spent the first seven years of my life in England. I expect my manner of speech has softened since then."

A flicker of approval finally graced Ivy's features. "As it so happens, I was also born in Gloucester."

While Cody chatted with Ivy about their mutual birthplace, Stephanie sidled over to Juliet. "Your grandmama is quite severe. I don't think she likes me at all."

"It only seems that way. Once you're on her right side, she's a wonderful ally."

Stephanie giggled. "My brother is trying to win her over already."

Although Juliet doubted Cody's attentions to her grand-mother would last long, when dinner was announced, he was quick to offer her his arm. "Would you do me the honor, Mrs. Beaucroft?"

A whisper of a smile lit the woman's lips as she gave him a nod. "Indeed, your manners *are* far superior to those of Lord Gryphon. Now that I look at you, I believe you may be infinitely more handsome."

Juliet exchanged a surreptitious, bewildered glance with Kitty. Their grandmother wasn't easily swayed, but Cody appeared to have made a positive impression on her. Juliet couldn't imagine why he would make such an effort with the irascible woman, unless he enjoyed tackling enormous challenges.

To his credit, Cody continued to be attentive to her grandmother throughout the meal, asking her opinion on various topics of conversation. In turn, Ivy told him amusing anecdotes about his grandfather, Lord Harkencester, whom she met in her first London Season.

"You oughtn't repeat this to anyone, Mr. Gryphon, but I rather fancied your grandfather over all the other gentlemen I'd met that Season. I would have encouraged him too, but for Mr. Beaucroft. My father was set on our marriage, you see, and I hadn't any choice in the matter. How is Lord Harkencester getting on?"

"Tolerably well, Mrs. Beaucroft. The next time I see him, I'll let him know you asked about his health."

"That would be lovely." Ivy's smile grew misty. "He might remember me better as the former Miss Ivy Landry. You favor him a bit, around the eyes."

Juliet was amazed. Cody had tamed her grandmother just as easily as he'd put his horse through his paces that afternoon. Perhaps Ivy was so charmed, she wouldn't ask any awkward questions about her engagement.

At the end of the meal, Kitty rose. "Ladies, shall we go through and leave the gentlemen to their conversation?"

En route to the drawing room, Ivy cleared her throat. "Juliet, perhaps you will show me where I can freshen up?"

Her heart sank at the news she would not escape interrogation after all. "Why, of course, Grandmama." She gave Kitty a meaningful glance. "We'll join you and Stephanie in a moment."

"Take your time. I'd like to confer with Stephanie on what

sort of activities and excursions we should plan, now that the gentlemen are here."

CHARADES

Once Kitty and Stephanie had disappeared into the drawing room, Ivy jerked her head toward the library. "Come along, dear. I need to have a word with you."

With the door closed, the older woman folded her arms across her chest and fixed Juliet with her shrewd gaze. "First Kitty, and now you? It seems both my granddaughters regularly practice deceit as a means to an end." As Juliet opened her mouth to respond, Ivy lifted a quelling finger. "And don't bother to dissemble, my girl. I know full well you aren't really engaged to Mr. Gryphon."

"I wouldn't have you think otherwise, I assure you, but I must ask you to keep my secret for now."

"But of course! Why else do I exist except to lend credence to your ruse?"

A sigh. "Please, allow me to explain."

"I'm giddy at the prospect of enlightenment."

Juliet explained the series of events leading up to the engagement and the aftermath.

"I meant to unwind everything after Stephanie accepted Augustus's proposal, but now there's to be another slight delay.

Since she's already fallen in love with him, however, it shouldn't be much longer."

"So this nonsense is just for Miss Gryphon's benefit?"

"I had my own selfish reasons, Grandmama. Because everyone expected Augustus and me to wed, had I not entered into another engagement quickly, I would have been seen as thrown over and somehow tainted. If you view things in that light, you'll see Cody's sacrifice is quite gallant."

"Gallant?" Ivy snorted. "The lad wants to see his sister wed to an earl."

Juliet was taken aback. "I had the impression you liked Cody!"

"I do like him—despite the fact his eyes are too wicked by half."

"Indeed they are." Juliet couldn't suppress a tiny smile.

"And what will people assume when your supposed engagement to Mr. Gryphon is broken? You'll be seen as tainted then, too."

"I-I'm afraid I really didn't think past the emergency." Juliet averted her eyes. "I may have to give up on the notion of matrimony. Now that I know how it feels to be drawn to someone, I couldn't settle for anything less."

"I assume you're referring to Mr. Gryphon?"

Juliet nodded. "The moment I saw him, I knew what had attracted Kitty and Philip to one another. If I can't have that in a marriage, I'd rather be a spinster."

"Then marry Mr. Gryphon." Ivy chuckled. "He's absolutely charming."

A shake of the head. "He's vowed to return to Texas after Stephanie is wed."

"You're a pretty girl, Juliet. Change his mind for him."

"That's not possible. He despises me."

An expression of incredulity came over Ivy's face. "Have you lost your senses? Between you and Kitty, I'd always assumed you held a modicum more intelligence! If Mr. Gryphon despises you, I'm a peahen."

When Juliet peered at her, uncomprehending, Ivy made a sound of impatience. "Why do you suppose he's spent the evening flattering me? It certainly wasn't for my good looks."

"I don't know, to be honest."

"He wished to please you, Juliet. It may have been unconscious on his part, but he could have had no other motivation than that."

"There's another explanation. He and I are both trying to act as if we're in love so Stephanie's fears will be assuaged. Ingratiating himself with you would seem to serve that end."

"Twist logic into a knot if you like, but the lad cares for you. If you care for him, you'll find a way."

"I'm not the heroine of a romance novel, Grandmama, and there will be no happy ending for Mr. Gryphon and me."

Ivy's lips pressed together into a line. "I, for one, refuse to believe it."

WHILE PHILIP and Augustus chatted in the dining room about issues regarding management of Grovebrook, Cody nursed his brandy. Although he found the conversation interesting, and occasionally offered a suggestion or observation based on his work on his father's ranch, he couldn't help but think about Juliet's attire that evening. Her crisp blue-and-white striped gown, although demure in all other respects, featured a lace-edged square neckline that displayed her creamy décolleté to its best advantage. In addition, the shade of blue she wore brought out the cerulean in her eyes and made him want to lose himself in their depths.

When would he have time alone with her, so he could properly tender his apology? Too many people were present that evening to discuss such a personal matter. Might she be interested in riding with him tomorrow morning before breakfast? Cody gnashed his teeth; at any mention of riding, his sister would want to come along. No, he'd have to enlist Augustus's help. No doubt the man would be eager to cooperate so he could have time alone with Stephanie.

At a lull in the conversation, Cody broached the topic.

"Lord Elbourne, would it be too much of an imposition if I asked you to monopolize my sister for a short period of time tomorrow? It's rather important I have a word in private with Juliet, and the two girls seem to be inseparable."

"It's no hardship at all, I assure you." Augustus frowned as he considered the matter. "I could ask Stephanie to sit for me after breakfast. I've been itching to sketch her likeness, and it's likely to take hours."

A broad smile spread over Cody's lips. "That would be perfect."

~

As JULIET and Ivy entered the drawing room, Kitty glanced up from her conversation with Stephanie. "Hello! We've just been discussing possible outings. Juliet, what would you say to going out on the water during your visit? There is a lake nearby with rowboats."

"I'd love it."

"On some other day we can ride to the vineyard to see how they press grapes," Kitty said.

"Exploring the shops in Grovebrook would be fun." Stephanie wrinkled her nose. "But perhaps that's an activity best left to the ladies."

"All those things sound marvelous." Juliet smiled. "It's too bad sheep shearing season is past or we could have watched the creatures lose their fleeces."

"Why don't you set aside a day for an outing at Drake Manor?" Ivy suggested. "I haven't any sheep, but I might suggest a fruit-picking party. My blackberry and raspberry bushes are full to bursting this year, and I can tell you firsthand my cherries are exceptionally sweet and delicious."

Stephanie gasped. "I adore cherries!"

"What a brilliant idea, Grandmama!" Kitty exclaimed. "And how kind of you to offer."

Juliet beamed. "Yes, it's terribly kind. I'm sure the gentlemen would also enjoy a fruit-picking party very much."

"Tonight, however, we're to have a little salon," Kitty said. "Everyone must contribute something—be it a song, a reading, or the recitation of a poem."

"When I invited myself for dinner, I didn't realize there were strings attached." Ivy grimaced and poured herself a glass of sherry.

To fill the time until the gentlemen arrived, Juliet sat down at the piano to play Mozart. As the soothing notes filled the room, however, she was reminded of some unfinished business. Although her visit at Constance Hall promised to yield all manner of delights, her duty to help Violet still weighed on her conscience. The longer she put it off, the more likely a planned outing would interfere. How was she to get away now?

As Philip, Augustus, and Cody sauntered in a few minutes later, Juliet broke off.

"Oh, please continue," Cody said. "I love music."

"Since Kitty has planned a salon for this evening, I'm glad to hear it. Once everyone has made themselves comfortable, Stephanie will sing for us first, and I'll accompany her on the piano."

Augustus brightened. "How splendid!"

Stephanie gave a little moan. "I'm so dreadfully nervous."

"I don't see why," Cody said. "I've heard you sing before, and your voice is nothing to be ashamed of."

"Singing for you and Papa is different. Nevertheless, I refuse to shrink from a challenge."

Once the gentlemen were settled, Stephanie crossed over to the piano. Juliet gave her an encouraging smile and whispered, "Don't forget, there are eight bars of music before you begin to sing."

"What if I forget the words?"

"Come stand behind me so you can refer to the page if you get stuck."

As Juliet played "Sleeping, I Dreamed Love," Stephanie sang. Her vocal performance was tentative at first, and her entire body trembled. By the time the Texian reached the chorus, however, she seemed to gain more confidence.

After the song was done, Juliet applauded along with the rest. "Beautifully done."

"Now, since you were first, you get to choose who goes next," Kitty said.

Stephanie's eyes danced. "Lord Elbourne, of course."

Augustus frowned as he contemplated the matter. "Hmm… I'll play 'Vive La Compagnie.'" He glanced at Philip and Cody. "If you chaps know the song, why don't you sing along? You can get your contribution to the evening out of the way."

Even though Kitty made a sound of protest, Philip shot to his feet. "Capital idea."

Cody laughed as he rose. "I'd love to."

The rendition of the classic was rousing and enthusiastic, and even Ivy was entertained. Augustus called on Kitty afterward, who played a ballad on the piano. For her offering, Ivy read a passage about love from 1 Corinthians 13.

Finally, Kitty stood. "Is there anyone who'd like to perform anything else?"

"I would. I've a recitation."

Cody stood, moved to the front of the room, and paused for several seconds, as if to prepare himself. Then he performed

Romeo's first monologue from the balcony scene in *Romeo and Juliet*. As he delivered his lines beautifully, and with passion, Juliet felt as if she were holding her breath. Yet in the midst of her admiration for his acting ability was an undercurrent of annoyance. His choice of a passage with a clear connection to her would have been flattering had he truly been in love, but he wasn't. Furthermore, his calculated attempts to endear himself to her grandmother all evening had been obvious, even to Ivy. Juliet wished to see his sister marry Augustus as much as he did, but didn't he realize his efforts in that regard had crossed a line? She wouldn't allow him to impose on her any further than he already had.

Heartfelt and lengthy applause greeted the end of Cody's soliloquy.

Stephanie practically glowed with pride. "My brother was in the drama club at university. Isn't he marvelous?"

"Indeed, he is. I could almost believe his performance was real." Juliet deliberately kept sarcasm from her response.

"Well, thank you all for participating in my little salon," Kitty announced. "You're wonderful sports and talented besides."

Ivy stood. "It was more amusing than I had anticipated, but I've a somewhat lengthy drive ahead of me. I'll say good night."

Kitty hastened over to kiss her on the cheek. "Shall we have our berry-picking party at Drake Manor the day after tomorrow?"

"I'll have my cook prepare a picnic."

"How exciting!"

"Cody, will you come with me to see Grandmama to her carriage?" Juliet asked.

"I'd be delighted."

"Philip and I should see Grandmama to her carriage," Kitty said. "We are the hosts, after all."

Juliet shot her sister a meaningful glance. "Please stay and tend to your guests. Cody and I would be honored if you'd let us play hosts in your stead."

A flash of comprehension came over Kitty's face. "Why, thank you, Juliet. That's most thoughtful."

~

As Cody escorted Ivy and Juliet from the drawing room, Stephanie hoped the older woman's departure wouldn't presage the end of the evening. While Augustus, Philip, and Kitty fell into conversation about the berry-picking party, she tried to devise another game to keep the fun flowing. When an idea popped into her head, she excused herself to go in search of Cody and Juliet, to enlist their cooperation. The front door was slightly ajar as she approached, and Cody's voice clearly audible outside.

"I'm glad we have a chance to be alone, Juliet, because I have something to say."

Stephanie paused. If her brother and Juliet were having a private moment, she didn't want to disturb them.

"Forgive me, but I must speak first."

The note of anger in Juliet's voice surprised Stephanie, and she edged backward.

Juliet continued, more loudly. "Your campaign to convince Stephanie of your passion for me is masterfully done, but you must rein it in." Unable to believe her ears, Stephanie froze. "If she believes you to be completely in love, how will she feel when you set sail across the Atlantic without a qualm? She'll know she's been duped, and won't ever forgive us."

Stephanie's temper flared, and she yanked the door open. Cody and Juliet turned toward her with shocked expressions.

"I came to see if you wanted to play charades, but I realize now we already have been." Tears blurred Stephanie's vision.

"You're my friend, Juliet. Cody, you're my brother. Why did you feel it necessary to make a fool of me?"

Cody looked stricken. "We haven't been trying to make a fool of you, I swear it."

"We only wanted you to feel as if Augustus was yours and yours alone." Juliet's voice had a note of desperation.

"D-Does Lord Elbourne know your engagement is a ruse?"

Her brother reached out his hand, as if in supplication. "Stephanie, he wanted to have time to court you properly. He couldn't do that if you thought his affections were already spoken for."

"Lies. All lies."

Stephanie edged backward and ran toward the drawing room. Augustus, Kitty, and Philip glanced up when she appeared, seemingly startled by her abrupt entrance.

"Did all of you know the engagement between Cody and Juliet was a ruse except me?"

Kitty and Philip exchanged an uncomfortable glance and Augustus blanched. Cody and Juliet rushed into the room, and then everyone seemed to be talking all at once. A wave of dizziness came over her and she felt like putting her fingers in her ears.

"Stop!" A heavy silence followed. "Lord and Lady Philip, I thank you for your hospitality, but I'm leaving here tomorrow morning." She gave Cody a scathing glance. "With or without you."

Heedless of propriety, Stephanie picked up her skirts, fled the room, and took the stairs two steps at a time.

IN TEARS, Juliet sank onto the nearest chair. Cody tore after his sister, and Augustus seemed frozen in place.

"The evening was progressing so well," Kitty murmured. "What on earth happened?"

Misery pressed down on Juliet like a huge, invisible thumb. "I was taking Cody to task outside for overplaying his role as ardent fiancé, and Stephanie overheard me." She glanced at Augustus. "I'm sorry. I never meant for it to happen."

"I know." He shook his head. "I encouraged your ruse to continue, so this is my fault more than yours. I should have had more confidence in my ability to woo Miss Gryphon on my own."

Juliet wiped moisture from her cheeks. "What should we do now?"

Philip cleared his throat. "It's best to let the storm pass, I think. Then, Augustus must start over with Miss Gryphon if he still wishes to make her his bride."

"I do." The earl frowned. "I just don't know how to rebuild her trust."

Kitty gave him a sympathetic look. "Take it from someone who knows, Augustus. You rebuild it one day at a time." She crossed over to her husband and melted into his arms.

Augustus nodded. "If you'll excuse me..."

As he left, the earl refused to look at Juliet. She could scarcely blame him. Not only had she helped ruin his chance of happiness just now, but she'd also destroyed her friendship with Stephanie. On a more visceral level, once the Gryphons departed Constance Hall, she'd likely never see Cody again. A knife seemed to pierce her heart, and she wasn't sure she could bear the pain.

She stood. "I think I'll retire."

"Perhaps things won't look as bleak tomorrow," Kitty said.

For once, Juliet couldn't even feign optimism. Without another word she fled upstairs, wondering if Stephanie would let her in if she tapped on the door. When she reached the corridor which led to her and Stephanie's rooms, however,

Cody was leaning against the wall next to his sister's door. He straightened as she approached and came to meet her, a wretched expression on his handsome face.

"She won't speak to me."

Juliet hung her head. "I'm so sorry. Part of me is glad she knows the truth, but, Cody, I…"

Almost of its own volition, her hand reached out toward him. He grasped it and pulled her into an embrace. In the next moment, he was kissing her lips as if he were a drowning man and she was air. She clung to him, even as tears squeezed from the corners of her eyes. Finally, he just cradled her in her arms.

"I had to kiss you one last time, *querida*."

"I'm glad you did."

Their lips met again, and Juliet never wanted his caresses to stop. Then, inexplicably, a dog whined at their feet. As Cody and Juliet looked down in surprise, Texas stared up at them, wagging her tail. Stephanie stood several feet away, a stunned expression on her face. Cody and Juliet sprang apart.

He cleared his throat. "I didn't see you there."

"The dog needs to go out." Stephanie shook her head. "What are you two doing?"

Juliet felt as if her head had been dipped into a cup of hot tea. "S-Saying good-bye."

"Yes, that's it exactly. We were saying our farewells." Cody's face was flushed a dull red. "Might not have another chance tomorrow."

"But I thought your engagement is a ruse."

"It is." Cody and Juliet spoke over one another.

Stephanie opened her mouth to say something, but then closed it again. "The dog must go out," she repeated.

"I'll fetch Robin Hood and go with you," Juliet said. "We'll let them out into the garden."

"Right." Cody gave them a curt nod and tugged on the sleeves of his jacket. "Good night, then."

"Good night," Juliet said.

He strode off down the hall and Juliet rushed to retrieve Robin Hood from her room.

~

WHILE THE PUPPIES watered the roses nearby, Juliet and Stephanie sat on a stone bench near the entrance of the garden with a lantern between them. Although Juliet was still horribly embarrassed about what had passed between her and Cody in the hallway, she forged ahead in an effort to mend her relationship with his sister.

"I understand how you might feel betrayed—"

"You don't understand at all." Stephanie scowled. "My father yanks me away from everything familiar and brings me to England to marry me off to a nobleman. Don't you think I see how everyone in London was sneering at me for my accent and strange manners? And then you come along, all perfect and ladylike and…*perfect*, and I feel like an ox. Cody admires you, Augustus draws your portrait, and I'm on the outside. And now I realize you've all treated me like a child with your silly games and pretend romances! How do you expect me to act?"

Juliet sighed. "Before you arrived, Augustus and I had assumed we would become betrothed. I confess, when I learned about the arranged marriage, I was very disappointed. In fact, I cried all night. That day on Rotten Row, I lied to you about my lost dog. I've actually never had a dog."

"I knew it!"

"I'm far from perfect. In fact, I was keenly disappointed not because of my adoration of Augustus, but because I wanted to marry better than my sister. I've always been jealous of Kitty."

Stephanie gasped. "You can't be!"

"Yes, I can. I know it speaks dreadfully to my character, but I must be honest with you."

"And all this time, I've been jealous of *you!*" She laughed. "If only we can get your sister to be jealous of me, we'll have come full circle."

Juliet giggled. "I think the best course of action is to be happy within ourselves. That way, we'll have no room for jealousy."

"I suppose not."

"At any rate, after I saw Cody, I realized something was lacking between me and Augustus. And after Augustus met you, he realized the same thing."

"Are you telling me the truth?"

"Augustus and I never even kissed. I'm not sure it even occurred to us."

"I can't say the same for you and Cody."

Juliet's blush returned. "I shouldn't have let your brother take liberties, but I couldn't seem to help myself. Please don't tell him I said so, but he's the most attractive man I've ever seen in my life."

Stephanie made a sound of disgust. "And yet he won't propose? This is why I advised you to steer clear of him."

"Yes, I know, but I don't regret anything. Next Season, I'll just have to look for a man who interests me the same way." Despite her words, Juliet didn't believe such a man existed.

"So you think I should give Lord Elbourne another chance?"

"Absolutely. I wish you'd give all of us another chance. We'll try not to let you down."

"Let me sort it out tonight and I'll let you know my decision tomorrow."

"Fair enough."

They called their dogs and returned to the house. As Juliet readied herself for bed, she hoped Stephanie would decide to stay at Constance Hall. If she did, however, Juliet wouldn't be able to look Cody in the eye ever again.

PRETENSE

When Juliet entered the dining room for breakfast the following day, Augustus, Kitty, Philip, and Cody were assembled, but Stephanie had not yet arrived.

Juliet nodded, careful to avoid Cody's gaze. "Good morning."

"Good morning," Kitty murmured.

Augustus gave her a wan smile, his eyes puffy from lack of sleep. Juliet slid into her chair without further conversation, and the room remained deathly quiet until they heard footsteps approach. When Stephanie sailed into the room, the gentlemen lurched to their feet until she was seated.

She picked up her napkin and glanced around the table. "Good morning." She paused. "I spoke at length with Juliet last night, and we cleared up some misunderstandings. Therefore, I've decided to stay."

The tension in the air evaporated. Cody's fist, which had been resting on the table, unclenched.

"I'm terribly relieved," Kitty said.

Juliet found she'd been holding her breath, and let it out slowly. "So am I."

"It would have grieved me terribly to have driven you away," Philip added.

"Yes, thank you for staying, Miss Gryphon," murmured Augustus. "I can't tell you how sorry we all are about what happened."

"After careful reflection, I've concluded your hearts were in the right place. Nevertheless, I don't wish to be deliberately misled again."

Cody shrank from his sister's level glance. "I wouldn't dream of it."

Stephanie's dimples deepened. "Well...I suggest we put this behind us for now."

As the meal progressed, Juliet noticed Cody was uncharacteristically subdued. In addition, he seemed as eager to avoid speaking with her as she was with him. The ensuing awkwardness was unavoidable, she supposed, but regrettable. The rest of their visit at Constance Hall would be strained unless they found a way to forget about the night before. Perhaps her journey to Little Brambleton would help put things in perspective...if Kitty remembered to invent some way to occupy Stephanie. Although Juliet would like to take her friend into her confidence, Violet's misfortunes weren't her secrets to tell.

"Our berry-picking party will take place tomorrow, but I've made no fixed plans for today," Kitty said. "Stephanie, would you care to show me how to make a corn husk doll this morning? I haven't any corn husks, but perhaps we might substitute strips of fabric. I'd love to describe the craft to my church circle."

Augustus glanced over. "Forgive me, Kitty, but might I request Miss Gryphon's company instead? I intend to sketch her likeness, if she'll agree to sit for me. I feel morning light is most conducive to a beautiful drawing."

Stephanie seemed pleased. "Why, I'd love to sit for you, if

you don't mind a few fidgets. It's difficult for me to be still for long."

"I'll let you move every fifteen minutes, but you're still allowed to breathe." He winked.

"Of course, I don't mind." Kitty slid Juliet a meaningful glance. "Stephanie and I can fashion corn husk dolls some other time."

Juliet seized her opportunity. "Philip, I've some errands to run in Grovebrook if I might borrow the gig?"

He nodded. "Absolutely. Well, Cody, would you care to accompany me to the church? Two of my tenants have a disagreement with one another, and I must mediate."

"Actually, I have a matter of pressing business this morning," Cody said. "I can't put it off any longer."

"I've some letters to write," Kitty said. "We're all happily occupied, then."

~

AFTER BREAKFAST, Juliet fetched her hat and handbag, and then went in search of Kitty. Her sister was alone in the drawing room, at the writing desk.

Juliet glanced around. "I'd expected to see Augustus and Stephanie here, hard at work."

"They're outside, sitting under the oak tree, and I couldn't be more pleased. How did you convince her to stay?"

"I had no choice but to tell her the truth." Juliet rolled her eyes. "I'm on my way to Little Brambleton. If I'm not back in time for lunch, please make some excuse for me."

"All right, but you really ought to take a maid along. Mama would draw and quarter me if she knew I'd allowed you to go alone."

"I've worn my dowdiest gown so people will take me for a

governess." She kissed her sister on the cheek. "Please don't worry."

Juliet hastened from the house, eager to catch the nine o'clock train. Philip had asked the coachman to bring the gig around, so she was on her way in short order. When she reached the station, she brought the gig to the nearby livery stable and paid the proprietor to care for the horse until she returned in several hours. Shortly thereafter, she'd purchased her ticket and waited on the crowded platform for the train to arrive. When it finally came to a stop, she hastened toward the back where she was more likely to find an empty compartment. Indeed, the very last one was completely unoccupied, and she settled in. After the train began to move, she breathed a sigh of relief. With no stops between Grovebrook and Little Brambleton, she had the compartment to herself and wouldn't have to make stilted conversation with strangers.

Not more than a half minute after the train left the station, however, a man appeared in the corridor outside and opened the door.

"Sorry, miss, but everywhere else is full. Do you mind if I join you?"

Shock registered on the man's face as he recognized Juliet. Although she was equally astonished, she managed to find her tongue before he did.

"You might as well sit down, Cody, before you're accidentally flung to the floor."

JULIET AND CODY stared at one another for several long, awkward seconds. If he weren't wearing an almost comically stunned expression, she would have thought he'd followed her onto the train. As it was, she was forced to conclude their meeting was an unhappy coincidence.

He sank down onto the opposite seat. "What are you doing here?"

"I might ask you the same thing."

"I'm on my way to Little Brambleton to speak with Violet Haver."

"That's me as well."

"Why didn't you ask me to accompany you?"

She bristled. "You're not entitled to know every bit of my business."

Although she'd thrown down a gauntlet, he chose not to pick it up.

"No, I suppose not." He shook his head. "You were right about Zachary. He's a bounder and a lout, and I don't think anything I said during our time together made the slightest bit of difference to him."

A pang of guilt made Juliet avert her gaze. "At least you tried, which is more than I've done for Violet. By now, I'm sure she's convinced I've abandoned her."

"If she's anything like my cousin, I don't blame you. Not anymore."

"There's one big difference between Lord Gryphon and Violet though, isn't there? She's to have a baby, whereas his only concern is himself." Juliet gestured toward her bag. "I brought a little money for her today, but I probably should have sent it right when I received her plea."

"You could still have sent it by letter. Why are you going to see her in person?"

"I wanted to assess her situation, and talk to her about ways she might support herself going forward. I've neither the means nor the inclination to send her funds regularly."

"Then you guessed I'd have no luck with Zachary?"

Juliet shrugged. "I'd like to think there's good in everyone, but I know it isn't always so." She met his gaze. "Why are you going to see her?"

"To apologize for my cousin, and to assist her financially. Since Zachary is the father of her child, I feel some sort of familial obligation to help."

Juliet stared out the window at the passing countryside. Cody was certainly a man of contradictions. His appearance was that of a gentleman, yet he'd performed the backbreaking work of a *vaquero*. Although he spoke with a proper English accent, his heart was in Texas. Virtual strangers earned his charity and concern, but she was apparently a passing fancy, easily forgotten. Was there something wrong with him, or was *she* to blame for her inappropriate attraction? She suspected the latter.

"I didn't mean to offend you last night with my soliloquy," he said. "I meant it as a compliment."

"I wasn't offended, but...I think you believe me to be cold and unfeeling. I'm neither, Cody. And since you're leaving England, I can't allow myself to be imposed upon."

It was his turn to stare out the window. Because his face had become a mask, she couldn't guess his thoughts. Nevertheless, she had plenty of her own to contend with. Last night, her grandmother had encouraged her to change Cody's mind about leaving. The man had made his desire for her plain enough, and she understood full well how to ensnare him with her charms. Nevertheless, she respected herself enough to wait for a man who loved her so unreservedly, he had no regrets about not choosing another life. Cody showed no signs of such devotion, and she refused to settle for anything less.

MRS. AGATHA DARIEN, great-aunt to Violet Haver, lived in a tiny cottage within a stone's throw of the train tracks. As Juliet and Cody stepped down from their hired carriage, they exchanged a troubled glance.

"I expect the occupants know the train schedule full well," Juliet murmured.

He frowned. "This is no place for a baby. He'll be deafened before he's three years of age."

Weeds choked the short swath of yard from the pavement to the front door. Since the brass door knocker had long been missing, Cody used his knuckles to rap on the wood. Moments later, Juliet heard Violet's voice from the other side.

"I'll get it, Auntie."

When Juliet's former friend opened the door, her gaze latched onto Cody. Her eyes widened and her skin grew pale. In the next moment, she sagged against the doorjamb.

Cody peered at her. "Are you unwell?"

"No. I'm sorry, but I thought you were someone else." She shifted her attention to Juliet. "So you've come after all." Violet tucked stray lock of hair behind one ear and stepped back to admit the visitors. "Please, come in."

The door opened into a vestibule, which led to a small parlor. Even though Cody had removed his hat, his head nearly reached the ceiling. When Juliet glanced up, she couldn't help but notice missing patches of plaster, likely shaken loose by vibrations from the passing trains. Although the residence was clean enough, it was in need of repair and maintenance, inside and out.

"Violet, this is Mr. Cody Gryphon, who is Lord Gryphon's cousin. Cody, allow me to present Miss Haver."

Violet curtsied before gesturing toward the sofa. "Do sit down." Her expression grew strained. "I know I ought to offer you tea and biscuits, but I haven't any of either. Please forgive me."

Juliet sat, wondering the best way to begin the conversation. Her friend wore a loose gown covered by an apron, but her garments couldn't entirely conceal her burgeoning waistline. Violet's face was fuller, and her hair far more simply arranged than Juliet was accustomed to seeing. Nevertheless, the woman's beauty was still very much in evidence, and perhaps even enhanced by her added softness.

Violet cleared her throat. "I'd introduce you to my aunt, but she's feeling poorly and keeps to her bed."

"I'm sorry to hear it." Juliet offered her a sad smile. "Forgive me for not coming to see you before now, but I wasn't exactly sure how to help." She glanced at Cody. "Mr. Gryphon went to see his cousin on your behalf, but I'll let him explain."

"Miss Haver, I'm sorry to tell you that despite my entreaties, Zachary was unmoved by your situation."

As tears sprang to Violet's eyes, he frowned. "Perhaps it's more accurate to say he treasures the memory of your affections, but I think he's lost confidence in himself. You see, he's also been disinherited by our grandfather, and is now earning a living by working with his hands. Zachary believes you may be better off without him, despite my remonstrations to the contrary."

"Poor Zachary!"

The tears spilled over, and Cody hastened to press his handkerchief into Violet's shaking hands. Juliet tried to keep her countenance, but she was confounded by her friend's tender sentiment toward the man who'd abandoned her. Her unwavering adoration in the face of such indifference drew Juliet's pity. Suddenly, her grievances against Violet seemed unimportant, and she was very glad she'd come to help. In addition, she was exceedingly glad Cody was here. She suspected his steady male presence was the only thing keeping Violet from becoming completely undone.

"I came to assure you of a certain level of financial support on behalf of my family," he said. "Your child is a Gryphon, after all."

Violet glanced up, a gleam of hope in her eyes. "Are you saying the Gryphons are prepared to accept me?"

Cody shook his head. "I've not been given permission to confide your situation to my immediate family, and I doubt very much my aunt, uncle, or grandfather would approve. Nevertheless, I feel it's the least I can do."

He retrieved a wallet from his inner coat pocket, extracted a large quantity of pound notes, and put them on the low table in front of Violet.

Juliet reached into her bag for the money she'd brought and laid her contribution on top of his. "I don't wish to be insensitive, Violet, but have you considered ways you might support yourself and the baby? You play piano very well. Perhaps you might give lessons?"

"I know you're trying to help, but how many good families will employ the service of a fallen woman? I've passed myself off as a widow so far, but I can't hide from the truth forever."

"There are many other ways to make money than catering to the gentry. Plenty of women have resorted to crafts, such as dipping candles, spinning yarn, or needlework."

"I suppose it's time to start planning for a future on my own." She gathered up the money and slid it into the pocket of her apron. "Since I've no pride left, I humbly accept your help." A sob caught in her throat as she met Juliet's gaze. "You've every right to despise me!"

"I don't despise you, Violet. You've your entire life ahead of you, with a beautiful child to care for. There will be challenges, but I expect you'll find your way through if you put your mind to it."

Juliet rose and gave her friend a kiss on the cheek. Thereafter, she and Cody took their leave and climbed into the waiting carriage. As they rode back to the train station in silence, he reached for her hand. Despite her vow to keep her distance from him, she was grateful for the physical contact. Her visit had underscored just how many blessings her own life held. At that moment, she wouldn't have traded places with anyone else on earth.

~

WHEN THE SOUTHBOUND train arrived promptly at eleven o'clock, Cody gave Juliet a smile.

"It looks as if we'll be back in time for lunch after all."

"Good. The fewer question we have to answer, the better."

They settled into a compartment, which they were once more fortunate to have to themselves. Cody was particularly glad to have privacy, since he had a great deal on his mind.

"I think I'll visit Zachary one last time, to tell him I've seen Miss Haver. Perhaps I can change his mind."

Juliet looked at him askance. "I don't suppose it'll do any good, but I admire your tenacity."

"I'm not sure what I was expecting to find in Little Brambleton, but Miss Haver is exceptionally beautiful. I intend to tell Zachary he's truly lost his senses."

She paused. "You were very good with Violet today. I quite admired your calm and kind manner."

"I admired your kindness as well." He frowned as he tried to formulate an apology. "I spoke out of turn before when I accused you of being hard-hearted. I'd had no call to say such a stupid thing, and I regret it."

Juliet gave a slight shrug. "It's forgotten."

He moved from his facing seat until he was sitting next to her, but she stiffened.

"Please return to your own seat, Cody."

His eyebrows rose. "I don't understand."

"Physical contact between us is improper and mustn't continue. I must implore you, as a gentleman, not to take liberties with me any longer."

Bewildered and somewhat hurt, Cody returned to his seat. "Have I done something to give offense?"

"On the contrary. I find my regard for you improves on closer acquaintance. Nevertheless, there's no future for us romantically. Therefore, we must remain disinterested friends."

Affronted, Cody folded his arms across his chest. So he was to be cast off like a hat or a pair of gloves, was he?

"You had no difficulty with my taking liberties last night."

"I thought you were leaving and I'd never see you again!"

He made a sound of impatience. "I know what you want from me, Juliet, but it's impossible. I've property waiting for me in Texas."

"Yes, you do, and I wouldn't dream of keeping you from it."

"I wouldn't dream of letting you!"

Even as the retort left his lips, he knew it wasn't entirely so. More than once he'd toyed with the idea of staying in England, with Juliet as his wife. But he kept returning to his love of open spaces, hard work, and freedom.

"I don't suppose you'd consider coming with me?" His question sounded almost facetious, but as he awaited her response he held his breath.

"And leave all my family and friends behind?" She shook her head. "No."

The sting of disappointment was rapidly followed by a flare of self-righteous anger.

"If you cared for me, you'd come."

"And if you cared for me, you wouldn't ask." Juliet's eyelids turned slightly pink as she struggled with her emotions. "Cody, thank you for even considering the idea, but let's agree it won't ever come to pass. Stephanie and Augustus will marry, you'll set sail, and I'll return to London next April for another Season."

"So you can be courted by an idiot like Mr. Waters?"

"I don't know." She stared at her hands. "I mightn't marry at all."

Cody wasn't sure what was worse: the image of Juliet in wedded bliss with that mealy-mouthed Waters, or as a spinster surrounded by cats.

"Cody?"

He glanced over to find her smiling at him. "Yes?"

"You might miss me a little at first, but by the time you've crossed the Atlantic, you'll be eager to get back to your ranch and begin the next part of your life. In the grand scheme of things, you and I will be a pleasant interlude which will be forgotten as soon as you meet your future wife. Let's enjoy the time we have together and not give flirtation another thought."

She turned her head toward the window, but not before a fat tear slid down her face. As she cried, Cody felt as if he was being turned inside out and pulled into a million pieces. Since he'd left his handkerchief behind in Little Brambleton, he had nothing to offer Juliet to dry her eyes. The symbolism suddenly struck him as perfectly ironic. He had nothing whatsoever to offer Juliet Beaucroft. Nothing at all.

THE MORNING of the berry-picking party dawned with such promise, Juliet knew the day would be one to remember. The ladies climbed into the carriage for the journey, while the gentlemen rode horses alongside. During her visit to Cousin's Cottage the previous day, Kitty had discovered Prudence was doing a little better and therefore she and Kirkham were added to the group.

The carriage paused outside their home for the viscount to see his wife to the carriage, and then mount his own horse.

Prudence's complexion had recovered its brilliance, Juliet noticed, and her good humor had rebounded as well. She'd equipped herself for the day with a wide broad-brimmed hat and had brought a pillow to sit on in the carriage.

"And I've left off my corset altogether," she confided, bringing her fingers to her lips.

Ensuing peals of delight from the other ladies brought Philip riding over to tap on the carriage. "Is everything all right in there?"

Kitty lowered the window long enough to shout, "Never better!"

The caravan passed through the village, and a few minutes later the train station was in view. Juliet was reminded of her intimate conversation with Cody the prior day and the emotional aftermath that had ensued. By the time they'd returned to Constance Hall, fortunately, she'd composed herself. As for Cody, he'd assumed such a polite, gentlemanly demeanor, it was as if nothing had ever passed between them. Pangs of regret haunted Juliet, but she tried to ignore them as much as possible. Never again would she enjoy the rakish flash of his mischievous eyes or the touch of his lips...but it was better this way for them both.

Although Kitty had given her and Cody a puzzled glance or two over lunch yesterday, she said nothing. Fortunately, Augustus and Stephanie were so wrapped up in each other, they didn't notice anything amiss. In the afternoon, Juliet found a moment where she could speak with her sister about Violet privately. To forestall any concerns, she related her serendipi-tous journey with Cody in an almost a humorous fashion, saving her more serious demeanor for Violet's plight.

"So Mr. Gryphon intends to appeal to his cousin's better nature once more?" Kitty shook her head. "I'm not sure Lord Gryphon possesses a better nature, but for Violet's sake, I hope I'm wrong." She peered at Juliet. "Have you and Mr. Gryphon quarreled again?"

Juliet forced herself to laugh. "Quite the contrary, really. We're getting along famously now that we've no silly ruse to promote. I like him very much and have every reason to believe he and I will be great friends for the remainder of his time in England." Considering her inner turmoil, she was surprised at how plausible her explanation sounded.

"I'm glad to hear he wasn't petty."

She waved her hand, dismissively. "Not at all. Cody apologized for speaking out of turn, and gave me credit for my kindly manner toward Violet. I assure you, our fellowship couldn't be more amiable."

"Do you think your attraction toward him has waned?"

"I'm embarrassed I ever mentioned it."

Indeed, Juliet *was* embarrassed to have mentioned it, since her attraction to Cody was raging worse than ever. She wasn't exactly sure why she wouldn't confide the truth of the matter to Kitty…except she didn't want her sister to resent the man for breaking her heart. Her sister would never understand Cody was already in love with the Republic of Texas.

Juliet was distracted from her reminiscences when Prudence began waving a silk scarf around. "I brought this along so we can play Blindman's Buff."

"What a wonderful idea! I love playing Blindman's Buff!" Stephanie exclaimed.

"Perhaps we all should have thought of a different game to play," Juliet said.

Kitty shrugged. "We can always play horseshoes, I suppose."

"I asked Cody to bring a length of rope." Stephanie's announcement was met with puzzlement. "I want him to demonstrate his expertise with a lariat."

Prudence's eyebrows rose. "That should be interesting." She paused. "Your brother looks an awful lot like Lord Gryphon, did you know?"

Stephanie laughed. "Indeed, several people have mentioned it."

"He's frightfully handsome, nonetheless. He should do well next Season, if he wishes to marry."

"Cody will likely return to Texas before then." Juliet gave Stephanie a mischievous glance. "Perhaps *long* before, should a certain happy event take place."

As Juliet had anticipated, her remark sparked conversation about engagement etiquette and customs, as well as the differences between weddings in Texas and those in England. A smile graced her lips all the while, but inwardly she felt like crying. If she could keep up this pretense of disinterestedness until Cody's departure, it would be a miracle.

IMPOSSIBLE

*C*ody had been so concerned about missing the train to Little Brambleton the day before, he'd barely paid attention to his surroundings. Today, as he rode ahead of Lord Philip's carriage, he was able to fully appreciate the beauty and charm all around him. Back home in the Piney Woods where his ranch was located near Nacogdoches, the land was untamed, largely covered with many different species of trees, and somewhat sparsely settled. Here in Grovebrook, however, the bucolic countryside had all been claimed and cultivated to some degree or another. Nevertheless, he enjoyed watching flocks of sheep grazing on emerald green grass. The fields burgeoning with wheat seemed to whisper as the wind rustled through the stalks. Albeit a tad too civilized for his taste, English countryside was admittedly lovely. Especially since it contained a particular English rose named Juliet.

For a few moments, he tried—and failed—to imagine her in Texas. A man with money could certainly purchase all the niceties a lady might expect as the wife of a rancher, but he couldn't duplicate the same sort of elegant society she had in

England. It might be different if he intended to live in New York City or even Farmington, Connecticut, where Stephanie had attended Miss Porter's School since it opened in 1843.

He glanced over at the viscount who was riding alongside him. "Lord Kirkham, Grovebrook strikes me as a very pretty place. How did Lord Philip come to be in possession of it?"

"Philip has always yearned to be a landowner. Since Grovebrook was one of the assets in his father's estate, he purchased it. And because Philip needed a man of business to collect rents and such, he offered the position to me. So far, we've been quite happy."

"I don't consider work to be beneath a man with a title, but my opinion seems to be in the minority."

"Perhaps, but I quite agree with you."

"If I'm not being too personal, how did you come to the same conclusion?"

The viscount gave him a broad grin. "When a man is deeply in love with a good woman, there's nothing he won't do for her." He cocked a thumb at his chest. "I'm such a man, and Prudence is such a woman. Since I've no estate, and only a pittance of an allowance, I'm obliged to make a living if I want to support a wife." He shrugged. "Truly, it's no sacrifice, and I rather enjoy being a useful person. In the end, I decided my life would have been meaningless without Prudence by my side."

Cody was touched by the man's story. "Thank you for being so forthright. Lady Kirkham is exceedingly lovely, and you're a fortunate man."

"I can't disagree with you there." Kirkham gave him a sidelong glance. "I understand Lord Moregate is interested in selling a few more underperforming assets from his estate. One never knows for certain which purchasers will put themselves forward, but among them might be another gentleman, like Philip, who wishes to become a landowner. If so, I hope he has just as much success."

"Yes. You've given me a great deal of food for thought."

The man's eyes gleamed. "Here's another crumb for your plate. Although Prudence thinks I haven't a clue, I've every reason to suspect I'm going to be a father."

Cody's eyebrows rose. "What good news! Congratulations are in order."

"Please keep it under your hat for now, since I'm not supposed to know."

"I'll be the soul of discretion, I assure you."

He laughed. "I thought my wedding day was the happiest day of my life, but this comes close. I can't help but wish the same felicity for every young man who is in love."

"Yes." Cody nodded. "We should all be so blessed."

Inwardly, he sighed. His purpose in acquiring property in Texas had been to own something tangible, to make his own way in the world, and to leave a legacy of achievement behind. Would any of that matter, however, if he couldn't share it with the woman he loved? Perhaps he was guilty of not seeing the forest for the trees.

JULIET'S MOOD improved immeasurably as she arrived at Drake Manor. She hadn't been to visit her grandmother in years, but had spent many pleasant summers here with Kitty when they were little. The square, three-story brick residence was not architecturally unusual, but it was imposing. The grounds were more interesting, with rolling green lawns, a lovely garden with a gazebo, and—of course—a rambling berry patch set next to a small grove of cherry trees. Juliet remembered full well the times she and her sister had stuffed themselves so full of fat, sun-ripened fruit, they'd been unable to eat dinner. Their grandmother had, fortunately, never taken them to task.

Ivy welcomed the carriage and riders with a beaming smile

as they arrived. Once everyone had assembled in the courtyard, their hostess gestured toward the house.

"I've set aside rooms where you may freshen up, if you wish. Afterward, servants will direct you to the party."

As they went indoors, Kitty gave Juliet a wink. "It looks as if Grandmama is enjoying herself already."

"I expect she doesn't get too many visitors anymore, so I'm glad we've come."

The day was quite warm, so Juliet left her shawl and gloves in the room set aside for the ladies. Stephanie, Kitty, and Prudence did the same, although the viscount's wife brought her cushion along.

A striped, open tent had been erected near the grove, and a trestle table with chairs positioned underneath. Servants stood by with moistened towels for the guests' hands. Although it was past breakfast and not yet time for lunch, another table had been set aside for refreshments. Pots of tea and pitchers of water were available, along with assorted biscuits and tiny sandwiches.

Although larger tubs had been arranged to receive pails of collected fruit, only four pails had been set out for the party-goers.

Ivy gave everyone a mischievous smile. "I thought for our first game, you'll form teams of two. Whichever team gathers the most fruit in the time allotted wins a prize."

Prudence squealed with delight as she plucked a pail off the table, grabbed Kirkham by the hand, and tugged him toward the berry patch. Stephanie happily chose Augustus, and Kitty tucked her hand around Philip's arm. As three couples strolled out from under the canopy, Cody gave Juliet an awkward smile.

"I'm afraid you're stuck with me, *señorita*."

Juliet saw no reason not to be gracious. "Then I have the best of the lot." She glanced at Ivy. "Will you join us, Grandmama? I hope the rules don't prohibit a team of three?"

But her grandmother waved off her suggestion. "Someone must be the disinterested judge, and that would be me. Run along and enjoy yourselves."

Cody picked up the remaining pail and offered Juliet his arm. "Shall we start in the cherry grove?"

~

JULIET CONCENTRATED on picking fruit from the lowest branches, while Cody was able to manage the ones higher up. For several minutes they worked without speaking at all, but the silence began to weigh on her. After a sidelong glance at her teammate, she cast about for an innocuous topic of conversation.

"Erm…have you seen the sketches Augustus made of your sister? I thought them terribly good."

"I quite agree. In fact, I'd like to have one of my own." He laughed. "Did Lord Elbourne mention my pathetic attempt at drawing? He came upon me just as I was making my first attempt."

"He didn't mention it, I'm afraid. Are you interested in learning to draw?"

"Not particularly, but I'd heard from a credible source that the most admirable gentlemen read, draw, and collect butterflies. Since I already read, and I'm not particularly keen on Lepidoptera, I thought I'd give drawing a whirl."

Juliet laughed and shook her head. Merciful heavens but Cody was charming when he wished to be! "Perhaps your credible source should have mentioned that the most admirable gentlemen pursue those activities most interesting to them… such as riding and trick roping, for example."

His eyebrows lifted. "Has Stephanie gone and spoiled my surprise?"

"Was she not supposed to say anything?"

"I didn't tell her not to mention it, but I didn't wish to excite anyone's anticipation. Trick roping can hardly be compared to the sort of artistic ability demonstrated by Lord Elbourne."

"He *is* exceptionally talented, but then I've rarely heard anyone deliver a soliloquy as masterfully as you did the other evening."

Cody sketched a graceful bow. "*Muchas gracias.*"

She giggled and redoubled her efforts to pick cherries. "I've no idea how long Grandmama means to give us, so we'd best not shirk."

"I wonder what could be the prize?"

"Whatever it is, if we win, I hope it can be split in two."

"I'll happily give my half to you, unless it's something dreadful. In that case, I'll take the entire prize for myself."

Juliet giggled again. "Perhaps it's a chamber pot."

"In that case, we'll have to arm wrestle for it."

Without warning, he caught her hand and drew her close. Although he said nothing, his eyes seemed to caress her face. When his gaze settled on her lips, her heart began to hammer in her chest and her resolve weakened along with her knees.

"Cody..."

His voice took on a note of desperation. "Do you care for me? I mean *truly* care for me more than any other man?"

She shook her head. "Please don't make me say it."

"Then say you despise me."

"I-I can't. It does no good to speak of my feelings."

"Then show me how you feel."

Cody leaned forward and pressed his lips to her in a long, lingering, burning kiss that registered in every part of her body. Afterward, he gazed into her eyes with a sad smile.

"Thank you, Juliet." He kissed her hand and then released it. "I just had to know."

"Whatever we have between us...you know it's impossible."

"Good. Love should be impossible, unforgettable, and maybe even a little dangerous. I'm not the sort of man to settle for less."

Ivy rang a bell just then.

"Our time's up," Juliet said.

Cody retrieved the pail. "For now."

As they hastened from the grove, Cody's cryptic remarks echoed through her mind. Was he speaking in riddles? She felt a flash of annoyance. The blasted man had forced her to reveal her feelings with that kiss, and she could never forgive him. In the next breath, her annoyance faded. No, no matter how much she wished to blame him, to do so was utter nonsense. She'd yearned to tell him he'd captivated her heart and had ached for his kiss. Strangely enough, now that she admitted her adoration openly, a sense of peace filled her soul. They might never marry, but to know he returned her sentiment was something she'd treasure the rest of her life.

CODY'S SPIRIT soared as he carried the pail of cherries back to the canopy. Ivy needn't announce the winner of the game, since he'd already won the most incredible prize. Juliet loved him. It would have been nice to hear the words, but her kiss had said everything he'd needed to know. None of the cherries he'd picked could have tasted sweeter than the joy spreading through his veins. In that moment, he didn't want to ponder the future; he just wanted to bask in the miracle that a woman as wonderful as Juliet could find something worthy in him.

As it turned out, Stephanie and Augustus returned with a pail overflowing with fat, luscious raspberries, and won a beautiful mosaic patchwork quilt for their efforts. His sister couldn't have been more pleased, of course, since she always loved to win. Prudence and Kirkham returned to the canopy with lips stained blue from eating fresh blueberries, and Kitty complained she and Philip couldn't pick fruit as quickly because they'd been chased away from their berry bush several times by bees.

Eager to spread his peacock tail feathers, Cody fetched the rope he'd brought and while everyone relaxed under the canopy, he demonstrated the trick roping he'd learned in Texas. As he dropped the lariat into a flat spin at his feet, he reveled in their rapt attention. When he spun the circle up and over his head, *oohs* and *aahs* made him smile. Then, after returning the lariat to its original flat spin, he spun it vertically and jumped back and forth through the circle several times. Once he'd demonstrated a few other maneuvers, such as spinning the rope while switching hands, he bowed, to great applause.

"Would anyone like to see how the lariat is used to capture animals?"

Stephanie raised her hand. "I would!"

Cody grinned. "Miss Beaucroft, might I beg your assistance to help me with my demonstration?"

Juliet's eyes widened, but she joined him.

"What should I do?" she whispered.

"Would you prefer to run or just allow me to rope you?"

"I-I'll allow you to rope me. I've no desire to run from you."

A ripple of pleasure made the hair on his upper arms stand at attention and brought a slow smile to his lips. "*Bien.* In that case, just wait here with your arms at your side."

Cody stepped out several paces, spun his rope into a flat spin, and then tossed it in a slow arc over Juliet's head. She gave a little squeal as the lasso tightened around her upper body, and then, amidst applause from the audience, he tugged her to him.

"You see? No struggle." Juliet laughed.

He loosened the rope and set her free. "I wouldn't say there hasn't been a struggle."

"What would you have done if I'd run?"

"Caught you, of course." He chuckled.

As Cody escorted Juliet back toward the canopy, people peppered him with questions about trick roping. During the ensuing conversation, Prudence rose.

"Kitty, will you accompany me to the house? I'd like to freshen up."

The two ladies hastened off. Augustus, Philip, and Kirkham wanted an impromptu lesson on how to perform a flat spin, so Cody demonstrating the flat spin technique. Since there was only one rope, Kirkham had the first turn. He'd just managed a reasonable rotation when Kitty returned with a frown on her face.

"Freddie, Prudence is asking for you."

Kirkham, upon noticing Kitty's unhappy expression, dropped the rope and ran toward the house. Cody exchanged a puzzled glance with Juliet. Prudence had seemed to be enjoying herself moments before. What could be amiss?

Kitty glanced at Ivy. "Grandmama, may Freddie and Prudence use your carriage to go home? She's feeling unwell."

"Of course." Ivy gestured to one of the servants. "Make sure the carriage is brought around, forthwith."

As the servant left, Ivy stood, took Kitty to one aside, and had a whispered conversation. As Cody watched, the older woman winced and shook her head. Moments later, Kitty and Ivy returned to the canopy.

"Please, everyone, do carry on. I must tend to Lord and Lady Kirkham just now, but I'll be back."

After their hostess departed, everyone stared at Kitty, hoping for an explanation.

"There's no reason for alarm. It's just that Prudence has had a bit of a disappointment, I'm afraid," she said.

Stephanie covered her mouth with her hand, and Juliet gasped. Although Cody suspected what had happened, Philip and Augustus looked bewildered. Kitty apparently noticed their expressions.

"Prudence had been hoping to present Freddie with good news, but she'll have to wait another month or two. There's nothing wrong, but the situation hit her rather hard and she became distraught."

Stephanie's face crumpled. "This is my fault. I should have kept my uninformed opinions to myself."

Augustus rested a comforting hand on her shoulder, and she rested her cheek against it.

Juliet glanced at the pillow left in Prudence's chair. "Should I take her cushion to the carriage?"

Kitty shook her head. "I think it's best to leave her and Freddie alone for the time being. I'll bring the cushion to Cousin's Cottage tomorrow."

The abrupt departure of the Kirkhams seemed to affect the atmosphere of the party immeasurably. As if on cue, clouds rolled in overhead and gave Drake Manor a bleak appearance. Stephanie proposed a game of Blindman's Buff, but Prudence had had the blindfold in her pocket and nobody suggested locating a new one. A game of horseshoes filled the time until luncheon was served, but Cody suspected nobody's heart was in it. Not even his sister seemed much interested in winning. After lunch, he managed to give a brief trick roping lesson to both Augustus and Philip before the outing came to a close.

On the ride back to Constance Hall, Cody rode three abreast with Augustus and Philip. When the two brothers chatted about future plans Philip had for Grovebrook, Cody was only half-attending. So much had occurred that morning, he could scarcely keep track of it all. The joy Juliet had brought him under the cherry tree had been blunted a great deal by Kirkham's disappointment. The viscount was a fine, jolly fellow, and it pained Cody to realize how he and Prudence must be suffering. Furthermore, when he thought about what his cousin was missing with Violet, he felt physically ill. Even a scoundrel was allowed happiness—if only he could be persuaded to seize it.

Although the caravan didn't stop at Cousin's Cottage, Cody felt the impact of the day's event anew as he rode past. Nothing but time and nature would cure Lord and Lady Kirkham's heartbreak, but that certainly wasn't the case with Zachary and Violet. He decided to depart Grovebrook for London tomorrow morning, so he could shake sense into Zachary. An inkling of a plan was beginning to take root in his mind, and he wanted to discuss it with his cousin. Above all else, he was determined to do the right thing for Juliet. The success or failure of Cody's meeting would impact whether he ought to return to Constance Hall or whether it was kinder to stay away.

IN THE DISTANCE, Stephanie shrieked with laughter as Augustus pursued her across the lawn. Juliet sat in the garden, alone and forlorn, while Texas and Robin Hood played amongst the ferns nearby. To her dismay, Cody had left that morning before she'd arisen, without any mention of his impending departure the night before. Instead of a personal good-bye, she'd discovered a letter from him slipped underneath her bedroom door. Although the missive was filled with warm sentiments about his regard for her, it contained few specific details about when she'd see him again.

After their cryptic conversation in the cherry grove at Drake Manor, Juliet had allowed herself to imagine Cody might have changed his mind about leaving England. Now, she feared he might have been indulging himself at her expense. If so, Juliet now knew how Prudence must have felt yesterday when she realized her fondest hopes had been dashed. If Cody Gryphon was truly cruel enough to lead her on, she could almost bring herself to detest him. Could the man's temperament really be so mercurial, or was her judgment fundamentally flawed where he was concerned? She picked up a walnut-sized rock and hurled it at an unsuspecting rosebush. A rose by any other name was a rake and she was a besotted fool.

Kitty emerged from the house and made her way toward Juliet's white marble bench. As the puppies ran to greet her, the brunette beauty knelt long enough to give them both a fond pat on the head and to let them lick her hand. Then she came to sit alongside her sister.

"I've just returned from calling on Prudence."

"How is she?"

"Feeling quite blue, I'm afraid, but I think she'll perk up in a day or two. It's *you* I'm worried about."

"I-I can't think what you mean."

"Yesterday, upon one of the occasions Philip and I were chased away from the berry bushes by bees, we decided to try the cherry orchard instead."

Juliet's face grew hot. "Oh."

"It's obvious you're in love with Mr. Gryphon, and he with you."

"We've not said so…not with words at any rate. But after he left today with only a short note of farewell, I must assume he's a rake who has intentionally misled me as to his feelings." She shrugged, even as her vision blurred with tears. "Of course, our sentiments are beside the point anyway. It's quite impossible to be in love with someone who lives on an entirely different continent." Hadn't Cody told her love should be impossible? Perhaps he truly meant it.

Kitty put a comforting arm around her shoulders. "Don't despair. I suspect Mr. Gryphon is only returning to London to speak with his cousin. You never know if he might not be at Constance Hall for dinner tomorrow night."

From across the grounds, Stephanie's giggles reached their ears.

Juliet gave Kitty a crooked smile. "Say nothing of this to Stephanie. She's so terribly happy with Augustus, I don't want my despondent mood to spoil things for her."

"I won't say anything whatsoever because I'm convinced there's nothing to say. Mr. Gryphon is a man in love, and a man in love can't possibly be parted from his lady for long."

"I'd like to believe you."

"Be of good cheer, Juliet. I have the feeling everything will work out for the best."

~

CODY ARRIVED at Lady Lovejoy's residence midafternoon, and discovered his father reading a book in the library. Horatio glanced up when he strode through the door.

"What are you doing here, Cody? Is anything amiss with your sister?"

"Stephanie's quite well, I assure you." Cody brought him up to date on recent events, including the fact his sister was aware he wasn't genuinely engaged to Juliet.

Horatio blanched. "I'm amazed she didn't insist on leaving Grovebrook, forthwith!"

"She nearly did, but Juliet convinced her our intentions were good. Fortunately, Stephanie and Lord Elbourne are getting along famously, and I would be surprised if they aren't engaged quite soon."

"Is that so?" His father visibly relaxed. "I'm exceedingly relieved."

"Have you found a house here in London?"

"Oh, er, I've suspended my search for the time being. You see—"

Lady Lovejoy sailed into the room just then. "Dearest, I've

received an invitation—" She broke off. "Why, Cody! I'd no idea you'd returned to town."

Although he tried to keep his countenance, Cody couldn't believe his ears. Unless the countess had been addressing the Greek statue in the corner, she'd called his father *dearest.* He slid a quizzical glance at Horatio, whose rosy complexion had turned positively ruddy. Furthermore, the man's tongue seemed to be stuck to the roof of his mouth. Had he nothing to say for himself?

Cody cleared his throat. "I'm in London on a matter of business, Lady Lovejoy, but I don't know for how long. Since all my trunks are still here, may I trespass on your kindness for a few days?"

"You're always welcome in my house, dear boy." The countess beamed. "I've begun to think of you and Stephanie almost like my own children."

A frozen smile covered Cody's shock and dismay. Despite his father's previous protestations to the contrary, apparently he and Lady Lovejoy had been getting along quite well indeed.

Horatio rose from his chair and took the countess's hand. "Lad, I suppose this is as good a time as any to say I've asked Adriana to marry me, and she's agreed."

The blood seemed to drain from Cody's extremities and his hands grew cold. "I-I wish you both every happiness."

His automatic and wooden response sent a wounded expression rippling across the countess's face, and Horatio frowned.

"I can understand your surprise, Cody, but there's no call to be rude."

"Forgive me if I've given any offense. If you'll excuse me, I have some business to attend to."

He bowed, hastened from the library, and climbed the staircase as if wolves were nipping at his heels. Simmering anger trailed in his wake. Nothing could have prepared him to see his father keeping company with the countess, however amiable and worthy she might be. His behavior reeked of disloyalty to his mother's memory, and Cody was glad Stephanie wasn't there to see it. Even as he strode down the corridor to his room, he admitted his resentment was, perhaps, unfair. Horatio was in the prime of life, healthy, and had been without female companionship for many years. Even so, Cody found the notion of his father remarrying abhorrent…if not positively revolting.

Nothing could induce him to stay in England now.

UNFORGETTABLE

Dressed in his old work clothes, Cody stood outside J. Morris, Butcher at closing time, waiting for Zachary to emerge. His cousin caught sight of him right away and sauntered over. Although the viscount looked as if he'd been eating more regularly, he still didn't seem to be happy. In fact, he appeared to be spoiling for a fight. If truth be told, so was Cody.

Zachary cocked his head. "You look as surly as I feel, cousin. What brings you around?"

"Dinner and a few pints."

"Slumming?"

"If it's good enough for you, it's good enough for me."

Zachary gave him a crooked grin. "Let's go."

They strolled through the streets of London, shoulder to shoulder, glaring at any young tough who looked at them sideways. After the third time, Zachary chuckled. "Ever been in a brawl?"

"A time or two. Texas is known for them."

"Sounds like my sort of place."

At length, they wound up at O'Shanty Tavern again, in a

corner booth. Cody curled his lip. "Tell me, Zachary, are there no other pubs in London?"

"It's not the finest establishment, but I know Angus, the barkeeper. More to the point, he knows about my little problem. Should my enemies be lurking outside, Angus would come to my aid."

"I guess that's worth something."

Cody choked down a small amount of fish stew before pushing the inedible repast away in favor of ale. Zachary finished his meal completely before draining his own tankard. They'd not exchanged more than a few words all night, but the viscount finally gave him an appraising glance.

"You didn't seek out my elegant company for no reason. What's on your mind?"

"I paid Miss Haver a call, at her great-aunt's residence in Little Brambleton. She's a beautiful woman."

Zachary averted his eyes. "Indeed, she is."

"I'll provide a dowry for Miss Haver, if you agree to marry her."

His cousin scoffed. "What could possibly prompt such generosity on your part? You don't know her and you barely know me."

"Because her child will be a Gryphon by blood. And... because Miss Haver is Juliet's friend."

"Juliet? You don't mean Miss Beaucroft, do you?" He shook his head in admiration. "If you've managed to woo her away from Elbourne, I'm impressed."

"There was no need to woo her away from the earl. Lord Elbourne is to marry Stephanie, and Juliet is very pleased at the match."

"And are you and Miss Beaucroft to wed, then?"

Cody frowned. "No. Look, I didn't come to talk about my romantic problems. I'm here to talk about yours."

"Who better to offer advice than somebody with nothing left to lose?"

"I don't need your advice. As soon as Stephanie is married, I'm returning to Texas."

Zachary seemed perplexed. "What's the allure of such a place?"

"In Texas, an ordinary man can build his own empire, if he's canny enough. I own four hundred acres of prime timberland near Nacogdoches. Once I've sold off some of the timber, I'll graze cattle and buy more land. I can't wait to leave England."

"If that be the case, why do you sound so bitter?"

Cody drained his ale and signaled the server to bring more. "I've just learned my father is to marry Lady Lovejoy, if you must know. The prospect fails to delight me."

Zachary seemed taken aback. "I know Lady Lovejoy rather well. Have you some particular reason to dislike her?"

"I don't dislike her at all. It's my father whom I resent for sullying my mother's memory!"

Zachary clucked his tongue. "Aunt Rebecca is gone, and your father is entitled to happiness. Return to your Texas empire if you like, but don't do it out of anger with Uncle Horatio."

The barmaid brought two more tankards of ale. Cody drank deeply, wiped the foam from his lips with his sleeve, and glared at his ale as if it were responsible for his woes.

Zachary shook his head. "Here's another bit of sage advice for you: don't cut off your nose to spite your face. If Miss Beaucroft cares for you, marry her."

"Ha! You're one to talk. A beautiful woman, who's having your child, is waiting for you. Instead, you choose to muck about in the underbelly of London—to what purpose? If you mean to punish yourself for past misdeeds, it's time to move on."

"Time to move on? I could say the same to you. Do you

really suppose your mother would want your father to be alone the rest of his days?"

"Leave my mother out of it."

"For that matter, would she want you to walk away from Miss Beaucroft out of some misguided notion of loyalty?"

Cody's eyes narrowed. "If you want to see just how well I can brawl, keep talking."

Inexplicably, Zachary laughed. "Two Gryphons in fisticuffs? That would be a sight to see."

The corners of Cody's mouth curled up at the edges, despite himself. "That it would."

The busty barmaid leaned over the table, the better to display her assets. "Can I get either of ye lads anything else?"

When they shook their heads, the woman straightened. "Ye don't know what yer missing." She sashayed off.

Zachary chuckled. "There was a day, not so long ago, when I would have taken the lass up on her offer." His merriment faded. "Are you in love with Miss Beaucroft?"

"It doesn't matter." Cody frowned. "Juliet won't leave England."

"Why should she? She hasn't lost everything, like Violet and I have. There's nothing here for either of us." He sighed. "I might be a devil, but my regrets will haunt me the rest of my life. Look at me, Cody, in all my pathetic glory. Don't end the same way."

Cody opened his mouth to argue, but Zachary cut him off.

"Your mother's memory lives within you, cousin. Not in Texas."

Deep down, Cody knew Zachary spoke the truth. As Juliet's beautiful face swam before his eyes, he realized he would have to let go of one dream to catch hold of a better one. Everything he wanted was in England, including the woman he loved.

He nodded. "You're right."

"Since I'm not often right, I'd best savor the moment."

Cody chuckled. "I have something more tangible for you to

savor, actually. It's the deed to my ranch in Texas. Once you've married Miss Haver, I'll sign it over to you. Take your wife to Texas, start your lives over, and establish your own empire. Her dowry will give you a means of support until the ranch begins to produce enough income on its own."

A gleam of hope lit Zachary's eyes. "Why would you do something like that for me?"

"Since I'm to have your inheritance one day, it's only fair I give you something in return. Make no mistake; the land is beautiful, but it's raw and undeveloped. It'll take a great deal of backbreaking work to make it productive."

Zachary glanced at his calloused palms. "I'm not afraid of hard work. But do you really think, after everything I've done, Violet will have me?"

"I've no doubt whatsoever."

His cousin smiled…and then he laughed. "I suppose I should clean myself up a bit before going to Little Brambleton, or I'll frighten Violet off." He rubbed the hair on his face. "I resemble a bear."

"You smell like one, too." Cody chuckled. "I'd recommend a hot bath, a shave, and a change of clothes, at the very least."

"What are your plans?"

"I'll buy some land in the English countryside, and marry Juliet. Not necessarily in that order, mind you."

"Thank you, cousin." Zachary reached across the table for a handshake. "Violet and I will travel to Gretna Green and return in a fortnight. Where can we find you?"

"I'm staying at Lady Lovejoy's residence this evening, but thereafter I'll be at Constance Hall in Grovebrook. That's where I'll propose to Juliet and pray she accepts."

"Don't take no for an answer."

"I won't." Cody dropped a handful of coins next to his empty tankard. "Shall we share a cab?"

"You go on. I'm going to devise a pretty speech for Violet, while I finish my ale."

Laughing, Cody settled his cloth cap on his head. "See you soon, then, and best of luck."

He left the establishment, feeling lighter than before. A grin spread across his face as he contemplated asking Juliet to marry him. No doubt she'd be a little vexed at him for his hasty departure that morning, so perhaps he ought to wait a few days—until she calmed down a trifle. On the other hand, maybe he oughtn't let the pot simmer overly long. If he rose early enough, he could catch the seven o'clock train north. Perhaps this time tomorrow evening, he and Juliet would be engaged—for real.

Several paces from the front door of O'Shanty Tavern, a man blocked Cody's path with obvious ill intent. Cody's eyes narrowed and he brought his hands up, ready to defend himself if necessary. "Step aside, sir, or it'll be the worse for you."

Oddly enough, the man chuckled. "I don't think so."

From behind Cody, somebody called out, "Gryphon! We'd like a word, if you please."

He turned to discover a trio of men approaching, none of whom looked familiar. How could they possibly know his name? "Are we acquainted?"

The shortest man chuckled. "Good one, Gryphon, but you've been hiding in the shadows long enough. Mr. Wickham sends his regards."

"I don't know a Mr. Wickham." A feeling of dread crawled down Cody's spine as he realized they'd mistaken him for his cousin. "You've confused me with someone else."

"The only one who's confused is you, for thinking you could cheat Mr. Wickham and get away with it."

The first man shoved him from behind, sending him directly into three pairs of fists. In the beginning, Cody did his best to return the punishment, but several vicious blows to the head sent him to his knees, reeling. Seemingly from a long distance off, he heard Zachary's voice, shouting. Thereafter, he lost consciousness completely.

～

THE RESIDENTS of Constance Hall returned from their outing at the lake in good cheer and my visit couldn't be more congenial. At least, that's what Juliet wrote in her letter to her parents. In truth, with Cody gone, she'd begun to feel like an outsider. Philip, Kitty, Stephanie, and Augustus made every effort to make sure she was included in each activity, of course, but she felt lonely just the same. Her cheeks were sore from the strain of smiling all the time, but she wasn't sure she was fooling anyone.

Juliet felt Cody's absence so keenly, she'd begun to reassess her priorities. He'd only been in London for two days, but how would she feel once he was parted from her for years? Perhaps she'd been stupidly foolish to discourage his addresses. Indeed, she was so much in love, she was increasingly doubting her resolve not to leave England. No, she couldn't bear to live without him.

On the other hand, how painful it would be for her to set sail across the Atlantic, able to communicate with her family only by letters which would take weeks or perhaps months to arrive? She'd miss the birth of Kitty's children, and those of Prudence and Stephanie, too. Her children would likely not meet their grandparents until after they were grown. All the joys of life, and the struggles that were sure to come, would be experienced only secondhand from both sides of the Atlantic. The prospect was unimaginable.

Either way she chose, heartbreak was sure to follow.

The third morning after Cody's departure, Juliet awoke, deeply unsettled. He'd failed to send a note to her or his sister, even to confirm he'd arrived safely. Although she realized there was probably little reason for worry, the lack of communication was remiss of him at the very least. Stephanie had mentioned her annoyance about it in passing, but she was too wrapped up in her relationship with Augustus to contemplate the oversight too much. Juliet, by contrast, had little to do but fret. Cody hadn't invited her to correspond with him, but she decided to write him a letter after breakfast anyway, just to inquire about his health. Surely her missive would prompt a response by return post, and set her mind at ease.

After Juliet was dressed, she and Stephanie went outside with their puppies, to let the little creatures into the garden for their morning activities.

Stephanie yawned. "Does Kitty have anything planned for today?"

"I think she mentioned shopping in Grovebrook. I'd like to pick up a present for my parents, if I can. Maybe something made by a local artisan."

"How thoughtful. Maybe you can find one of those beeswax candles Kitty mentioned?"

"Oh, yes, that would be perfect. Perhaps I'll also buy a jar of honey for Papa. He loves honey on his morning toast."

A loud gurgle made Stephanie laugh and she patted her stomach. "Speaking of toast, I'm starving!"

Juliet laughed. "Peckish, do you mean?"

"That's it, exactly."

They left the dogs to play in a fenced-in section of the garden and returned to the house for breakfast. Augustus, Philip, and Kitty had already assembled in the dining room, and Juliet felt guilty. "Good morning. I'm so sorry to have kept you waiting."

"I'm sorry, too," Stephanie said. "The puppies needed to go out."

Kitty smiled. "Please be seated and don't give it another thought. I was thinking about going into Grovebrook today.

The only question is whether or not we should ride or take the carriage." She glanced around the table. "Any thoughts?"

While they were debating the issue, the morning post arrived. As was his habit, Philip sorted through the mail first. Moments later, he held up an envelope. "Miss Gryphon, you've received a letter."

She brightened. "It must be from Cody! I can't imagine why it took him so long to write."

The letter was passed down to her, but when she examined the envelope, a frown appeared. "It's from Papa. Why would he write to me, but not Cody?"

Juliet bit her lip. "It's probably nothing, but why don't you have a look? Nobody minds."

Stephanie flashed a brief smile. "Well, if you're sure..." She opened the letter and began to peruse the contents.

Juliet's heart leaped into her throat when Stephanie gasped.

"Papa writes to say Cody's been hurt!"

A wave of dizziness was followed by a deep chill all the way to Juliet's soul. "Go on, Stephanie. Please."

"There was some sort of fight, but Papa doesn't give any details. He says Cody was knocked unconscious and they aren't sure if he'll wake up! He's at Lady Lovejoy's home." As Stephanie rose to her feet, her napkin slid to the floor. "I must go to London without delay."

Augustus stood. "I'll escort you."

Philip rang for a servant. "Pack an overnight bag for Miss Gryphon and for Lord Elbourne, and have the carriage brought around. They're to depart Constance Hall immediately."

"Yes, Lord Philip." The maid curtsied and hastened off.

Kitty gave Stephanie a worried glance. "If you hurry, you should be able to catch the nine o'clock train."

"Thank you!" Without another word, she ran from the room.

Juliet shot to her feet. "I'm going, too. Kitty, will you take care of Texas and Robin Hood?"

"Of course. Don't worry about a thing. Philip and I will bring the puppies and the rest of your things to London later today."

"Bless you." Juliet bit back tears as she dropped her napkin on the table and fled upstairs to get ready.

As the train sped south, Juliet wished it could sprout wings and fly. In the seat facing her, Augustus held Stephanie's hand. Her friend's pretty features were tight with worry, and Juliet was certain hers were as well. Never before had she faced the prospect of a mortal injury to someone she loved, and all sorts of dire thoughts stampeded through her mind like panicked horses.

Stephanie had read and re-read her father's letter over a dozen times, hoping it contained information she'd overlooked somehow. Even now, she was trying to parse the tersely written sentences to decipher what they meant.

"What sort of fight could Cody have been involved with?" Stephanie shook her head. "It makes no sense."

"I expect it has something to do with Lord Gryphon." Juliet's voice sounded as taut as a violin string, even to her own ears.

Both Augustus and Stephanie peered at her with bewildered expressions.

"How could Zachary be involved?" Stephanie asked.

"A former friend of mine was cast out by her family in disgrace. Her ruination was at your cousin's hands, and Cody was attempting to convince him to marry her." Juliet clenched her hands in her lap more tightly, to keep them from shaking. "Unfortunately, Lord Gryphon has fallen into a bad crowd."

Stephanie gaped. "You knew Cody's efforts would put him in danger, and yet you let him go anyway? That's unforgivable!"

"Cody's not the sort of man who can be told what to do! In

point of fact, I discouraged him from the attempt, but he was too decent to agree with me." Juliet averted her eyes. "Nevertheless, if it makes you feel any better, I hate myself worse than you could possibly imagine." Try as she might to maintain control, rivulets of moisture slipped down her cheeks. "I should have told Cody I love him, but I never did."

Augustus cleared his throat. "Don't give up hope, Juliet. You may still have the opportunity."

Tears filled Stephanie's eyes. "I-I shouldn't have spoken to you in anger just now. I'm worried about my brother. None of this is your fault, so please don't hate yourself."

Although Juliet gave her a tremulous smile, her self-loathing increased that much more. Why had she shown Violet's letter to Cody in the first place? She should have just sent money to the girl and let it go at that. In the next moment, a feeling of shame swept over her. Could she really have lived with herself by ignoring Violet's desperate plight so completely? In truth, she'd shared that letter with Cody because deep down she'd known he had the integrity to do something about it when she didn't. He'd made her a better person by his actions, but at what cost? Juliet prayed she would be able to tell Cody how she truly felt. Furthermore, if he still wanted her, she would go with him to the ends of the earth.

A DEEP VOICE called his name. "Quit loafing and open your eyes, Cody. I haven't got all day to wait for you to wake up."

Cody wished his cousin would go away and let him return to his bower of blackness, but unfortunately, the man kept talking.

"You must think yourself quite lordly, to have everyone at your beck and call in this manner. I'm beginning to think you the most selfish creature ever born."

With an enormous effort, Cody lifted one swollen lid and

gave Zachary what he hoped was a baleful glare. "Hold your tongue." He was surprised he could even form words, since his lips didn't seem to want to function properly.

His cousin hastened to his bedside. "Oh, good, I've annoyed you into regaining consciousness. It's fortunate for you, I daresay, since I was preparing all manner of insults. I was going to play the Minister's Cat of Abuse. Frankly, I could have gone on with it for some time. I've learned all manner of foul epithets in the slums."

Cody focused on Zachary's clean-shaven face. "You've lost your beard."

"And picked up a few bruises. I look positively rakish with my new black eye, and I think I may have broken my nose."

As Cody peered at Zachary's visage, the man's nose did appear to be swollen. The noise emanating from Cody's throat was meant to be a chuckle. "Good. You won't look like me anymore."

"It is *you* who resembles me." Zachary laughed. "I'll go fetch your father. He and Lady Lovejoy have been out of their minds with worry."

"Wait." Cody paused, trying to muster the energy to speak. "What happened last night? I don't remember anything."

"It was the night before, actually. Mr. Wickham's thugs had been sent to kill me, only they mistook you for me. Angus alerted me to trouble and then I jumped into the fray. Fortunately, Angus followed up with a lead pipe and chased off your assailants. He helped me get you into a cab, and I brought you to Lady Lovejoy's. She's been quite hospitable, and let me have a bath. Actually, I think she required it as a condition of my residency." He glanced down at his gentlemanly attire. "I hope you don't mind if I borrow your clothes."

"Not at all. I owe you a debt of gratitude for saving my life."

Zachary shook his head and guilt twisted his bruised and swollen features. "You owe me nothing, Cody. It never occurred to me you'd be in any danger, and I tender my most sincere apology." He took a deep breath. "Now, excuse me while I summon your father. I had an accidental moment of moral clarity just now, and I didn't enjoy it." His cousin punctuated his sentence with an exaggerated shudder.

Ordinarily, Cody would have laughed, but he was in far too much pain. After Zachary disappeared, he retreated back into darkness.

DANGEROUS

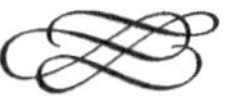

It was late afternoon when Juliet, Stephanie, and Augustus arrived at Lady Lovejoy's home. The two girls rushed inside while Augustus paid the cab driver. Stephanie grabbed the butler as he came to meet them in the entryway. "Yeats, is my brother all right?"

"Er…I believe he's sleeping, Miss Gryphon, but more than that I can't say."

Augustus entered the home and gave his hat and traveling cloak to the butler. "Would you be so kind as to have our bags brought in?"

"Right away, Lord Elbourne."

Zachary descended the stairs just then, and Stephanie peered at him in shock. Juliet was also taken aback, but for a different reason. The man's ordinarily handsome features were battered, his eye sported a purple circle, and his nose was swollen. A laceration covered the knuckles on his right hand, and from the way he was moving, she surmised his muscles were sore.

"For a moment, I thought you were Cody!" Stephanie exclaimed.

"You must be Stephanie." He managed to bow, although it

brought a wince to his face. "I'm Zachary Gryphon, your cousin." His gaze flickered toward Juliet. "Miss Beaucroft."

She executed the briefest of curtsies. "Lord Gryphon."

Stephanie's eyes narrowed as she peered at him. "Was it you who hurt my brother?"

"Not directly, but I admit, I inadvertently put him in harm's way. His assailants believed they were exacting revenge on me, you see."

Augustus didn't bother to bow, but merely gave him a level stare. The two men regarded one another with mutual disdain.

"I can't say I'm glad to see you, Elbourne."

"Likewise."

Juliet's patience was at an end. "Take us to Cody, please."

Zachary's lips tightened and he jerked his head toward the stairs. "Come along and I'll show you to his bedchamber. The physician just left, and Uncle Horatio and Lady Lovejoy are visiting with him now."

As they ascended the stairs, Juliet couldn't hold back the question that had been burning into her soul since she first heard Cody was injured.

"Lord Gryphon, h-how is he?"

Zachary waited until they'd all reached the landing before he replied. "Cody was beaten badly. I had a dickens of a time getting him to wake up at all, but we had only one lucid conversation before he slipped away again. The doctor advised us he's fortunate to be alive."

Stephanie gasped and clung to Augustus's arm. Tears stung Juliet's eyes anew, and she had to touch the wall to steady herself.

Zachary showed them to the wing of the house reserved for gentlemen, and gestured toward an open door on the left hand side. "He's in there, but don't expect much. As I mentioned, he's asleep almost all the time."

Juliet and Stephanie hastened toward the door, just as Lord

Horatio and Lady Lovejoy emerged. The older man gave a sigh of relief when he saw his daughter.

"Thank heavens you've come." As he enfolded her in his arms, she burst into tears.

Juliet gave the countess a worried glance. "May I see Cody, please?"

"Why, of course, dear. As Mr. Gryphon's fiancée, you've a perfect right to be by his side."

Evidently, Cody hadn't yet informed Lady Lovejoy the engagement was a ruse, but Juliet didn't bother to correct the misunderstanding. "Thank you."

The countess touched her arm. "Brace yourself."

Juliet rushed into Cody's room, and her eyes riveted to the figure lying prone on the bed. Although the heavy velvet curtains over the windows had been partially drawn, enough late afternoon sun seeped through the opening to make lamps unnecessary. As she crept closer, the extent of Cody's injuries made her want to weep. His lips were swollen and split, and his battered face was covered with black and purple bruises. A knot was visible on one temple, and a cut on his eyebrow was encrusted with dried blood. The white coverlet on the bed had been turned down to his waist, revealing bandages wrapped around his ribs. Lacerations and purple shadows covered the knuckles on his hands, and a smattering of black smudges marred the skin on both arms.

Her horror was so great, Juliet didn't even notice when Lord Horatio, Augustus, and Stephanie joined her in the room. Cody's sister came to stand on the opposite side of the bed, and as she stared at him, a moan was torn from her throat.

"My poor brother!"

"The doctor said he has several badly sprained fingers and some broken ribs," Horatio said. "Cody managed to sip a little water when last he woke, and we gave him a few drops of laudanum then. He's been sleeping peacefully since."

From the doorway, Lady Lovejoy spoke. "There's nothing you can do for him right now. I'll have a servant show you to your rooms, and perhaps we can all have tea."

Juliet scarcely heard when Augustus mentioned he'd be leaving for The Aerie after tea, to welcome Philip and Kitty when they arrived that evening. When the countess finally called her name, she glanced up. Everyone else had already filed out of the room, and she was the only one remaining.

"May I stay here, Lady Lovejoy?" She pointed to a chair. "I just want to sit with Cody awhile longer."

"Of course, dear. I'll have your things taken to your room and a maid will bring you tea."

"You're very kind."

Once the older woman had disappeared, Juliet shoved the chair a little closer to the bed and positioned it so she could catch every movement Cody might make. Before she sat, she bent over his face, wishing there was some unbruised part of his visage upon which to deposit a gentle kiss. Thwarted, she pressed her lips to one of his uncovered shoulders before draping her soft, light shawl over his upper body to ward off any chill. After removing her hat, she settled into the chair and gazed at Cody's profile. She meant to be there when he woke up.

OVER THE NEXT THREE DAYS, Juliet could be induced to leave only long enough to change her clothes and wash her face. Otherwise, she ate very little and slept sitting up in the chair next to Cody's bed. Philip and Kitty stopped by to deliver Stephanie's puppy and to check on Cody's progress, but there was little to tell. He was unconscious most of the time, and when he stirred, he was barely able to sip some water before dozing off.

Stephanie had another chair brought in so she could also keep a vigil. While the former Texian attempted to embroider a screen—to please Lady Lovejoy, she claimed—she kept Juliet apprised of the news.

"Zachary went off to Little Brambleton this morning, to elope with his amour," she said. "The silly man insisted on waiting to leave until the swelling of his nose had receded to his satisfaction."

"Your brother must have persuaded him to marry Violet, then." Juliet glanced at Cody's profile. His bruises had begun to change color and take on more of a yellowish tortoiseshell look. "I doubt if anyone else could have managed it."

"There's also another engagement to announce."

Juliet stared at Stephanie, startled. "Are you and Augustus to wed?"

"Alas, it's not our engagement. Not yet, anyway." She giggled. "To my surprise, Lady Lovejoy and Papa are to be married."

"Really? How do you feel about that?"

"I confess, it took me a little while to get used to the idea. But I think the countess must love Papa a great deal. She told me that years ago, she'd preferred Papa over Lord Lovejoy. Unfortunately, her parents wished her to marry an earl."

"I've heard much the same story from my grandmother about her marriage. It's a common tale, I fear."

"The countess sacrificed the love of her life to make her parents happy, so her relationship with Papa now strikes me as rather touching. I just wonder if she'll be giving up any of her social status after they wed."

Juliet's gaze flickered to Cody's face before returning to Stephanie. "A woman in love is willing to give up a great many things—for the right man." She paused. "I might as well tell you now; Cody asked me once before if I would be willing to go with him to Texas. At the time, I refused, but I've since changed my mind. If he'll have me, I want to go with him when he leaves England."

Cody fidgeted then, and murmured something Juliet couldn't hear. Instantly, she and Stephanie were by his bedside.

"What is it, Cody?" Juliet asked. "Would you like some water?"

He shook his head ever so slightly. "I said, it's too late. You and me. Texas. Too late."

Juliet straightened. "I-I understand." But Cody had already drifted off again.

Bitter disappointment welled up within her, like dark red blood from a deep cut, and she suddenly felt as if she'd fallen into a hill of ants. The great revelation she'd had about her feelings for Cody had been for nothing, it seemed. Cody's fancy for her had passed, if indeed it had ever genuinely existed, and she'd made a complete and utter fool of herself.

She glanced at Stephanie. "I believe I've overstayed my welcome."

The Texian looked aghast. "Oh, Juliet, I'm certain Cody didn't mean it! Surely it's the laudanum talking."

"He hasn't had any laudanum today."

"Perhaps we misunderstood him, then."

"You heard what he said as well as I did." Juliet edged toward the door. "He doesn't want me after all." She swallowed the lump in her throat. "Please, stay with him. I really must go, but I'll pray for Cody's speedy recovery."

Distraught, she fled to her room and rang for a maid to pack her things. She planned to take a cab to The Aerie to spend the night. First thing tomorrow morning, she and Robin Hood would go home to her parents, where she belonged.

~

As Juliet entered the drawing room at The Aerie, Robin Hood came scampering over. Kitty put down her knitting and hastened to give her a warm welcome.

"Mr. Gryphon must be a great deal better if you've come here!"

Juliet managed to smile. "Yes, he's on the mend, I think. I hope you don't mind if I spend the night? I'm going home tomorrow."

"You are?" Kitty's eyebrows rose. "You really wish to leave before Mr. Gryphon is on his feet?"

"He's in very good hands, I assure you, and I seem to have developed an advanced case of homesickness." She picked Robin Hood up in her arms so she could stroke his fur. "How has the puppy been getting along in my absence?"

Her sister gave the dog a fond glance. "He's quite the most winsome creature. I'm surprised he and I have got on so well."

"Keep him, if you like." Although she was dying inside, Juliet forced her tone to remain lighthearted. "I daresay Mama and Papa will be glad when I arrive home tomorrow without him." She put the dog down.

Kitty frowned. "Is everything all right? You seem strained."

"I'm a bit worn out, actually. If you don't mind, I'd like to lie down."

Her sister rang for a maid to escort Juliet to her room. There, she sat down at the desk and wrote Lady Lovejoy a note, thanking her for her gracious hospitality during the recent crisis involving Mr. Gryphon. She also wished her every happiness on her engagement, and closed with a mention of her leaving town. Thereafter, she wrote a short missive to Stephanie regarding her departure, giving her the same excuse of homesickness she'd given Kitty. When the letters were sealed, she gave them to a servant to deliver the following day, and asked not to be disturbed until morning.

Those tasks completed, Juliet closed the drapes, threw

herself down on the bed, and let the storm of sorrow envelope her completely.

～

WHEN CODY OPENED HIS EYES, he felt significantly better and far more focused than he had in a long while. He began to move parts of his body, trying to assess the damage. Two fingers on his left hand were terribly sore, but he didn't think they were broken. He couldn't say the same for his ribs, however, but that particular injury seemed to be the worst. Fortunately, his headache had finally disappeared, and he felt relatively human. He vaguely remembered having a conversation with Zachary, but he had difficulty deciding if it was two hours ago, or yesterday. Somewhere along the line, he'd heard Stephanie and Juliet talking, but he couldn't recall if he'd managed to speak with them at all.

Although it took him several tries, he managed to sit up and put his legs over the side of the bed. As he did so, he suddenly felt ravenously hungry. How long had it been since he'd eaten anything? Gingerly, he got his feet on the floor, rang for a servant, and sank into a chair to wait.

At length, a footman appeared. "How are you feeling, sir?"

"Rather the worse for wear. Might I have something to eat… preferably something soft?"

"Yes, Mr. Gryphon. Breakfast will be served soon. I'll bring you up a tray."

"On second thought, I think I'd like to go down. Will you help me dress?"

"Of course, sir."

Twenty agonizing minutes later, Cody was dressed, but his clothes felt terribly loose. Worse, his reflection in the mirror struck him as exceedingly grotesque. He only hoped he'd managed to do some damage to his assailants before he'd been knocked unconscious. From the bruises on his knuckles, it seemed as if he had meted out a fair bit of punishment.

The footman prepared to leave. "Is there anything else, Mr. Gryphon?"

"Ask my sister to pop in before she goes down to breakfast, will you? I'll wait here."

"Yes, sir."

The fierce growl of Cody's stomach was apparently audible even to the servant.

"Er...there's a biscuit jar on the dresser table, Mr. Gryphon. The biscuits were baked yesterday."

"I could eat the jar whole." Cody chuckled. "You might have just saved my life."

He'd wolfed down two biscuits and was nibbling on a third when Stephanie hastened into the room. "You're finally awake! I must say, you're a sight for sore eyes."

"Please, don't mention the word *sore* right now. How long have I been out?"

"Let's see...this is the fourth morning since I arrived, and I think you were unconscious for two days prior."

His jaw dropped. "Are you joking? No wonder my pants are so loose!"

"I'd never joke about something like that. We've all been horribly worried, especially—" She broke off. "Would you like me to help you downstairs?"

"I'm not sure. Now that I've had a look at myself, perhaps I'm not fit to be seen. I wouldn't want Juliet to recoil in horror."

"She's not here."

"Oh? I thought I heard her voice while I was in bed."

"Juliet left yesterday, actually. She's staying with Kitty and Philip, at Augustus's house."

"I confess, I'm a little disappointed. I'd hoped to speak with her today."

Stephanie's shoulders moved up and down in an awkward

shrug. "I think you already said too much, Cody. I know she wouldn't want me to tell you, but she's heartbroken."

He shook his head, bewildered. "What did I say? If I babbled on about another woman or something, it was because I was out of my mind."

"You don't remember, then." She sighed. "Juliet was telling me she'd changed her mind about going with you to Texas, and you interrupted to say she was too late."

"I did? Well, it is too late. After Zachary returns from marrying Miss Haver, I've promised to sign the deed to my ranch over to him. He and his wife are going to Texas and I'm staying here to marry Juliet."

She inhaled sharply. "Is *that* what you meant? Oh, Cody, it sounded as if you were saying it was over between you. Her face went white and I thought she would faint!"

Cody groaned. The notion that he'd caused Juliet pain—however inadvertently—made him recoil inside.

"Help me downstairs, please, so I can beg the use of Lady Lovejoy's carriage. I'll visit Juliet this morning and make things right."

Once he and Stephanie had reached the ground floor, however, the butler presented her with a letter.

She bit her lip. "It's from Juliet." She slit open the envelope and read the missive. "She's leaving for her parents' home in the country this morning."

"I can't let her leave town thinking I've thrown her over." He frowned. "There's no time to waste. I'll take a cab and catch her before she leaves."

"But you haven't had breakfast and you can barely move!"

"Food isn't important right now, and as long as my lips can move, that's all that matters."

∾

THE RAVAGES of Juliet's crying jag made her cringe away from the mirror. She'd no desire to eat breakfast, but if she didn't make an appearance, Kitty, Philip, and Augustus would worry. Of course, as soon as they saw her swollen face, red nose, and bleary eyes, they would know something was horribly wrong. She sighed and buried her face in a moist washcloth in an attempt to ameliorate the damage. If only she could go to breakfast wearing a heavy veil!

When a maid came to help her dress, Juliet asked for a traveling suit in bottle green—hoping the color might counteract the pink of her face.

"Oh, and I'll like to wear a hat with a veil on the train."

She couldn't wear the hat to breakfast, unfortunately, but at least the veil would allow her to travel without suffering the indignity of curious glances. Just as the maid was pinning her hair into a simple chignon, there came a knock on the door. When Kitty appeared, Juliet forced a smile to her lips.

"Am I running late? I'm awfully sorry."

But Kitty wore worried expression. "No, you're not late, but Mr. Gryphon is in the drawing room. The poor man can barely walk and he can scarcely breathe. I nearly burst into tears at the sight of him."

Stricken, Juliet stared at her sister. "Why is he out of bed?"

"I don't know, but he wishes to speak with you badly enough to drag himself here." Kitty peered at her. "I don't know what disagreement has passed between the two of you, but I beg you to settle it. You both look as if you've passed into purgatory without any hope."

WHEN JULIET ENTERED into the drawing room, Cody was sitting on a sofa, in obvious pain.

"For mercy's sake, Cody, what are you doing here? You're not well enough to be moving around this way."

"There's been a horrible misunderstanding between us, and I can't let it go on. I've given my Texas property to Zachary, and I'm staying in England—if you'll marry me, that is."

Juliet peered at him. "*That's* what you meant before?" As she realized the extent of her mistake, her knees gave way and she sank onto the sofa next to him. "I-I don't know what to say."

"I didn't plan to propose to you looking like I was dragged down ten flights of stairs by my face. Nevertheless, you should know I adore you, *mi querido amor,* and I desperately want you to be my wife."

She shook her head and laughed. "This is impossible."

"What?"

"You said before that love should be impossible, unforgettable, and maybe even a little dangerous, and that's exactly what we have. You just asked me to marry you, but in your current condition, we can't even kiss."

He scratched his head. "That wasn't what I meant at the time, but I quite completely agree. Definitely impossible."

"Absolutely unforgettable."

"And terribly, terribly dangerous." Cody gave her a sidelong glance. "You could, however, say you'll be my bride."

He reached out his hand, palm up, and she rested her hand in his.

"I will."

His swollen lips formed the semblance of a smile. "Now that we have that settled, there's one more thing you could do for me."

"Anything."

"Feed me breakfast."

TWO OUT OF THREE

The ballroom at Lady Lovejoy's residence was filling rapidly with guests arriving for the wedding break-fast. Since the church could only accommodate a certain number of people, not everyone at the breakfast had been at the wedding ceremony itself. Any invitation to one of Lady Love-joy's events was cause for elation, however, and few people felt slighted.

As Juliet sat at a table with her friends and family, she surveyed the crowds with amazement. "I can't believe Lady Lovejoy convinced so many of her friends to return to London for a wedding in the dead of winter."

Stephanie laughed. "An intimate affair for two hundred fifty of her closest acquaintances."

"It's a testament to her social clout," Kitty said. "The countess has always been a force to be reckoned with."

"Cody and I have been given permission to call her Adriana. I did offer to call her Stepmother, but she refused." Stephanie giggled. "She said the name of stepmother made her feel like a wicked old crone."

Her brother smiled. "Since Adriana makes Father happy, I'll call her anything she wishes."

Kitty glanced at Prudence, whose hands were folded over her burgeoning stomach. "Are you entirely comfortable?"

An expression of concern crossed Kirkham's face as he regarded his wife. "Yes, dearest. We can have a servant bring you a pillow, if you like."

"No, that's not necessary." Prudence waved aside their concerns. "I'm feeling perfectly marvelous, I assure you. Actually, I wish to hear the news from overseas. I understand Juliet has had a letter from Lady Gryphon."

"Yes, indeed." Juliet nodded. "Lord and Lady Gryphon have had a healthy baby girl, and are settling into their new home fairly well. Violet writes that she had a little trouble understanding the local accent at first, but she's doing better now."

"No doubt Lady Gryphon will soon learn to ride astride." Augustus gave Stephanie a wink.

"Hush!" She glanced around to make sure nobody but the guests at their table had overheard him. "You're never going to let me forget that, are you?"

"No." The earl grinned. "The thought still intrigues me."

"Let's just call it a youthful indiscretion and leave it at that, shall we?" Stephanie gave him a level look. "A countess would never do such a thing, or so I'm told."

"We'll find out in April, after we're wed." Augustus's expression reflected the joy he felt inside.

"You must promise Cody and me faithfully you'll be back from your honeymoon in time for our wedding," Juliet said. "I wouldn't want you to fall in love with Europe and forget to come home."

Augustus chuckled. "There's absolutely *no* chance of that."

"I quite agree." Stephanie gave the earl a fond glance. "Augustus and I wouldn't miss your wedding for anything."

Liveried servants began to wheel food-laden carts into the room as they prepared to serve the first course.

Kitty frowned. "Where can Philip have gone? He said he wished to speak with one of the guests, but he should have been back by now."

Kirkham glanced around. "There he is now, walking this way alongside an older gentleman." His lips parted in surprise. "Oh, my." He lurched to his feet.

Puzzled, Prudence followed her husband's gaze. "Why, it's Papa! Why didn't Mama tell me he'd come with her?"

Everyone at the table stood as Philip approached with Lord Trestlebury at his side. The older man nodded his acknowledgment to one and all, but he crossed to Kirkham and sketched a bow. "You look well, Frederick."

"I've never been better, sir." As the viscount returned the bow, Kirkham wore a barely concealed expression of astonishment at his father-in-law's newfound cordiality. "As you may have been told, Prudence and I have every reason for good cheer."

"So my wife said." Trestlebury regarded his daughter for several moments before bending forward to deposit a kiss on her cheek. "I confess, when your mother told me that I was to become a grandfather, I was terribly proud."

Her eyes shone with emotion. "I'm so glad, Papa."

"I'd best return to my own table for now, but perhaps you might reserve a dance for your stubborn father later on?"

Prudence's happiness lent her countenance a serene beauty. "Of course."

Lord Trestlebury nodded one last time before he strode off in between the rows of tables.

After he left, Augustus stared at Philip in shock. "You must have said something very clever to have him come to his senses in this fashion."

"You've worked a miracle," Prudence added as she exchanged

a tender glance with her husband. "Our baby will come to know his grandfather, and that means everything to me."

"Indeed, Philip, we can't thank you enough," Kirkham said.

"I wish I could take the credit, but I can't. Trestlebury approached me to apologize for his bad-tempered response to the elopement. Then, he insisted on accompanying me to my table so he could make amends to Kirkham and Prudence." Philip shook his head. "I don't know why he changed his mind, but I had nothing to do with it."

"Then it was the baby who worked the miracle." Prudence smiled. "The least among us was the most powerful."

Kitty lifted her water glass. "I propose a toast to babies. Two in this year alone."

Juliet frowned. "Technically, Violet's baby came last year. New Year's Eve, actually."

"I'm not referring to Lady Gryphon's child."

Kirkham wrinkled his forehead in confusion. "You're not trying to suggest Prudence is expecting twins, are you?"

"Not of which I am aware."

Philip peered at his wife, his hand shook, and he nearly dropped his glass. "You don't mean to say...that is, are you telling me...?"

A smile played around Kitty's lips. "I am, indeed. You're to be a father."

Fortunately, the ensuing burst of excitement at the table was subsumed by the general hubbub in the room. As Juliet grasped her fiancé's hand under the white linen tablecloth, all she could think was how happy she was at that very moment. She met Cody's gaze and gave him a slow smile. All traces of his ordeal had long since faded, except for a minor scar across his left eyebrow. Despite that, she thought him the most wickedly handsome man she'd ever seen.

He leaned over to whisper in her ear. "'Heaven is here, where Juliet lives.'"

She gave him a teasing glance of appreciation for the quote. "You know Shakespeare personally?"

"Oh, yes, William and I are very close. He was going to entitle that particular play, *Cody and Juliet,* but I expressly forbade it."

"Why?"

"Because the play he'd written was a tragedy. In our case, however, we live happily ever after."

"Perhaps our love isn't quite so impossible after all."

"No, but it's still unforgettable." His gaze dropped to her lips. "And oh, so dangerous."

"Two out of three isn't bad."

"Not bad at all."

Heedless of prying glances or impertinent remarks, Cody and Juliet kissed.

The End

SNEAK PEEK AT THE GLASS HEART

After Merrill's widowed mother becomes engaged to an earl, the fate of their respective estates hangs in the balance. A battle of wits ensues when the earl's arrogant son shows up to make demands. Despite their prickly start, once Merrill discovers she and the viscount have both been painfully crossed in love, she begins to feel a measure of empathy. Unfortunately for their burgeoning relationship, a tempestuous drama threatens to tear them apart forever.

Keep reading for an excerpt...

EXCERPT FROM THE GLASS HEART

When Merrill finally loosed her last arrow, it sank into the red center with a satisfying thwack. She was puzzled to discover the muscles in her arms and back were shaking, until she remembered she'd been practicing for over three hours. She stretched out her arms as she strode toward the target to retrieve her arrows. "Practice makes perfect, as they say."

On her return, she noticed the portly butler approaching with an uncharacteristic frown on his face.

She cocked her head. "What is it, Northam?"

He presented a silver salver containing a card. "Lord Wharton has arrived."

"I've never heard of the man." Merrill peered at the engraved card made of heavy parchment, upon which was written, *The Right Honorable, The Viscount Wharton.* "What a bother." She dropped her arrows into the quiver stand and stripped off her leather arm guard. "I suppose I ought to receive him."

"Perhaps I should have said he intends to stay." Northam wore a pained expression. "He brought a considerable amount of luggage as well as his valet."

"What?" Merrill was taken aback. "That's absurd!"

Northam nodded. "I insisted nothing be unloaded from the carriage until I spoke to you."

"You did quite right. Ravenell is not a hotel, for mercy's sake."

Merrill lifted her chin as she strode toward the house. As she approached the drawing room, she was dismayed to hear the sound of piano music — a song from Gilbert and Sullivan's *The Gondoliers*

"Cheeky devil," she muttered.

Despite her irritation, Merrill plastered a serene smile to her lips as she sailed into the room. A young man was sitting at the baby grand piano and she was obliged to raise her voice to be heard. "Excuse me?"

Lord Wharton broke off playing and rose to his feet. "You must be Miss Cawthorne? Good afternoon." He picked up a snifter of amber liquid from the piano lid and lifted it up as if in a toast. "Thank you for making me feel welcome here at Ravenell."

Despite his words, the man's eyes glittered with obvious and inexplicable dislike.

"If I *have* made you feel welcome, it was entirely inadvertent." Merrill returned his glare with one of her own. "You've not been invited, so what is the meaning of this intrusion?"

"Forgive me but I *have* been invited — by your mother," With his left hand, Lord Wharton extricated a letter from his jacket pocket. "This letter of introduction is addressed to you."

As Merrill crossed the room to pluck the letter from his fingers, he swirled the amber liquid with appreciation. "I usually don't drink before dinner, but this brandy is lovely."

She bristled. "It's Armagnac from Gascony, and it's a very rare vintage."

"Mmm." He took a long swallow. "*C'est magnifique.*"

Merrill discovered the letter was in her mother's hand and

did indeed appear to be a letter of introduction. She read the entire missive through twice before glancing at her unwanted guest.

"You are Lord Seacombe's son, then." Merrill gritted her teeth. "I am to show you every courtesy."

Lord Wharton bowed. "I am delighted to meet you, Miss Cawthorne — or should I call you sister?"

"We are not related yet, so Miss Cawthorne will do." She peered at him. "Why have you come?"

He put the snifter down so hard she thought he might have broken the stem. "In contemplation of marriage to your mother, my father may sell his estate out from under me."

"That's unfortunate, sir, but what does that have to do with me?"

He fixed her with his gaze. "In contemplation of marriage to my father, your mother may sell Ravenell instead."

Merrill gasped. "What? No!"

"It will be one or the other. Neither my father nor your mother have decided yet."

"That's not possible."

"It is not only possible, but from what I overheard, they have indicated the sale of one estate is a certainty." Lord Wharton's eyes narrowed. "If we do not find a way to stop this travesty of a union, one of us will be deprived of our home."

ABOUT THE AUTHOR

 Originally from Southern California, Suzanne G. Rogers currently resides in beautiful Savannah, Georgia on an island populated by exotic birds, deer, turtles, otters, and gators.

ALSO BY SUZANNE G. ROGERS

HISTORICAL ROMANCE

Graceling Hall Series

Larken (Book One)*

Lord Apollo & the Colleen (Book Two)

The Vanishing Beauty (Book Three)

The Beaucroft Girls Series

Ruse & Romance (Book One)*

Rake & Romance (Book Two)*

The Mannequin Series

The Mannequin (Book One)*

Grace Unmasked (Book Two)

The Star-Crossed Seamstress (Book Three)

A Chance of Rayne (Book Four)

The Substitute (Book Five)

The Gilded Age Series

Duke of a Gilded Age (Book One)

Lady of a Gilded Age (Book Two)

Standalone Titles

A Gift for Fiona

Spinster

Lady Fallows' Secrets

My Fair Guardian

Jessamine's Folly

The Ice Captain's Daughter

Rumer Has It

An American in Paris of the West

Courtship on Eaton Square

One Little Kiss

The Prettier Sister

The Glass Heart

*Available in audiobook format

ALSO BY SUZANNE G. ROGERS

FANTASY

<u>The Yden Series</u>

The Last Great Wizard of Yden (Book One)

Dragon Clan of Yden (Book Two)

Secrets of Yden (Book Three)

Kira (Prequel to the Yden Trilogy)

<u>Standalone Titles</u>

Dani & the Immortals

*The Dragon Rider's Daughter**

Clash of Wills

Tournament of Chance: Dragon Rebel

Magical Misperception

*Whimsical Tendencies**

Something Wicked in L.A.

Royal Promenade

*Available in audiobook format